The White Tree

The White Tree

Mark C. Brown

Books of Brown
2018

First Printing: 2018

ISBN 978-1-387-37738-1

Books of Brown
Ellicott City, Maryland 21043
USA

booksofbrown@gmail.com

Dedication

To my loving wife, Naisha

With all the fantastical places we can visit
And people we can meet
You are my most beautiful reality
With whom I get to share love, life and laughter

Acknowledgements

First, and foremost, to God, who has given me the ability and inspiration to write. Thank You for blessing the work of my hands. The glory is always Yours.

To my wife Naisha, who gave me the time to write, and rewrite, and rewrite again. You gave inspiration and direction too.

To my mother Elizabeth, and to my sister Angela, who read each chapter as I wrote it, and gave me feedback.

To my son AJ, who invested in designing the cover. Great job!

To Lorraine, who took it upon herself to read, proof and edit this book. *(To Rob too, who let me 'borrow' his fiancé to do the work).*

To Ron, for the dragon *(everyone needs a dragon).*

To movies such as Star Wars, The Lord of the Rings. Indiana Jones and The Chronicles of Narnia. Always an inspiration.

CONTENTS

Chapter 1

❧ THE JOURNEY ❧

His breath on the window made it fog up. Cade's head was resting on the train window. He drew a little happy face with his nail bitten finger then wiped it away with his hand, as he let out a sigh. His normally optimistic sky-blue eyes were tired, contoured now with a touch of redness, looked up at the grey soaked clouds that blanketed the overcast sky, blotting out the warmth of the sun's rays. The day was chilly and it was raining. In fact, it had been raining ever since he got off the plane.

Cade slumped back in his chair and twisted his neck from side to side, as he yawned. The cabin car he was travelling in had emptied out at the previous station, so he stretched his long torso out while running his fingers through his wavy brown-black hair. The journey had been long. Two planes, a coach, and now a train ride. Being nearly seventeen, Cade had travelled from the U.S to the U.K by himself and now was heading toward Wales. He thought he had seen the last of Wales ever since he had moved with his dad to the United States of America over a year and a half ago. His dad, Bryce, a professor of sorts, was a little eccentric. He was, of all things, a relic hunter. Everything and anything to do with the Dark Ages whet his appetite, luring him into a quest, to discover and uncover, all he could find. What drove Cade's dad's interest into the Dark Ages was a mystery to Cade ever since he was a small boy. However, for as long as he could remember, it was all his dad ever talked about.

Bryce Evans, a Professor of the Dark Ages and Medieval Times and Practices. His quest-driven passion had made him very knowledgeable about many things, but his main love was the life of the Dark Ages! Of course, without question, he loved his son dearly. Bryce had raised him from a baby, pretty much on his own, but in growing up his son never warmed to this love of 'history' like that of his father.

Sadly, Cade did not know much about his mother. She had disappeared many years ago when he was roughly two years old. Being that young, he had no real memory of her, only the faint whispers and shadows of echoes past, drifting like shifting vapors. That was over fourteen years ago, and throughout that time, his father never really spoke much about her. All Cade knew was that a search had gone on for months, but to no avail. It was a very heartbreaking and sad time. Shortly after her disappearance, Cade's father, began to bury himself in learning, finding a reassurance from history. Consequently, the Dark Ages became a passion of his, a passion that Cade did not fully understand.

The jolt of the train stopping roused Cade from his thoughts. Llandyke Wells, last stop. He looked out of the window, at least now it had stopped raining. There were not many people around, maybe half a dozen or so. Llandyke Wells was a small village, consisting mainly of local village folk and farmers.

Cade stood to collect his things from the overhead luggage rack - a backpack and a suitcase - and made his way towards the exit. He stepped down from the carriage car onto the platform and looked left and right. The skies were grey, the air wet and the smell of the rain still hung in the air.

The railway station was a small grey/black flint stone building; the kind you see on old-fashioned picture postcards. In fact, the whole place looked like a step back in time. The town of Llandyke Wells was all made mainly of the same kind of stone, since there used to be a stone quarry a few miles away, long since abandoned, from which most of the town was built.

Surrounding the town were a few small farms and cottages scattered here and there, thinning out as you traveled further from town. Open fields, woodlands, forests and rivers were the main backdrop that stretched on for miles.

The only thing that stood out was Byne Keep, upon Glynn Hill, in the distance. It stood there broken, wounded over time, ravaged by fire, its authority of long ago, an ancient past in ruin. Now, overrun with plant and wildlife, long forgotten by the locals, it was a playhouse for many a kid that ventured out there.

A taxi was waiting for Cade outside the train station. The driver held a handwritten sign that said, 'Evans'. Cade walked up to the driver and said, "That's me".

"A'ight laddie" the driver replied, "Welcome to Llandyke

Wells.", nodding slightly as he touched the brim of his flat cap, "'Ere lemme take that for you", he continued, taking the suitcase.

Cade opened the back passenger door, climbed in and sat down while the driver put his suitcase in the boot of the car. After Cade buckled in the seatbelt, he took out his earbuds from the side pocket of his backpack and put them in his ears, hit play on his Smartphone and listened to some streaming music on Pandora.

The driver returned to his seat, looked over towards Cade and said, "You ready?", but Cade paid no attention, his mind was on his music, "a'ight laddie" the driver said with a slight smile and chuckled to himself, turning his eyes back to the road. He started the car and drove off.

Cade had been here before; he grew up here. Up until the age of seven, the town of Llandyke Wells and its surrounding fields and farms had been his home. After that, he and his dad moved south into a bigger, more city-like town, away from the rolling country hills of Wales and into the hustle and bustle of city life. This life, Cade loved. Aberandoen was a completely new lifestyle for Cade, one that he quickly adapted to. The sounds, the noise and the buzz of the city were all different, compared to the life had he grown up with. Here was television, music, telephones, mobile phones, computers and people. People were everywhere. There were probably more people living in one apartment building than in the whole town of Llandyke Wells.

It is hard to imagine living in the twentieth century without all the modern technology, but if you never knew about it, you could not miss it. Being only seven at the time, Cade was not missing much. He had learned so many things like fishing and hunting, planting and farming, and horse riding.

Growing up on a small farm was hard work, for everyone. Even though Cade was young at the time, this did not excuse him from the daily chores of farm life. Eggs had to be collected from the chicken coop, the pigs had to be fed, the stables had to be cleaned out and the cows and goats had to be milked. This life was a life that belonged to his grandparents and still did today. They had lived there all their lives and raised a daughter there too, his mother.

Nevertheless, that was the kind of lifestyle Cade and his dad left behind. Cade soon forgot about the simple way of living and became very astute in today's technology that now surrounded him. It fascinated him. It was a different world, one he wanted to master. Unlike his father who had a passion to learn everything about the Dark Ages, Cade had a passion of his own, to learn everything about the digital world, the Digital Age as it were.

School was a new experience for him too, since he had always been homeschooled Nonetheless, Cade found himself excelling in almost every subject. It had almost become too easy for him, science and technology were his greatest strengths. From junior school to senior school, Cade was top in his class, and even in the entire school; this enabled him to jump a few grades, not really making him the most popular kid, but that did not matter, Cade just busied himself with the latest computer gizmo. He had built dozens of computers, his first one being when he was only nine years old. That made him money too. He would build them then sell them for profit, using that money to buy more parts and/or the latest gadget.

With each passing year, Cade grew in stature. He was taller than his dad (who was only five foot three), his features were softer and he was leaner too. Cade did not inherit the brawn and roughness of his father's strength, but he had the strength of a learned mind, one that was disciplined but inquisitive, a trait they both shared. The ironic thing was it seemed like he and his father were two polar opposites, both passionate to learn all they could, driven and dedicated in the craft of knowledge, however one looking at the past, the other looking at the future.

There were other things that they had in common too - food and travel. Cade's father, Bryce, could rustle up a meal fit for a king with only a few ingredients. Bryce and his son would often challenge each other in a food cook-off, using the same ingredients to see who could come up with the best dish. Until recently, Bryce would win but Cade's determination was beginning to show; he had won the last two competitions and was planning for a third.

Being the kind of man Bryce was, meant that he never stayed still for too long. That is why they had moved to Aberandoen. Traveling to and from the city was much easier and quicker than it was traveling from Llandyke Wells.

When Cade was still a young boy, they would only travel during the summer months, just visiting parts of England where it required only a short train ride, where they could be back within the same day. Other times, they would camp out for days at a time, which Cade loved. The quick flip-up tent made it so easy to set up and settle down for the night. His father would then tell stories of long ago, about life during the Dark Ages and how they were living like they did, off the land. However, this was not strictly true. They would bring their own canned food, soda and water to drink, with a camp-out kit for cooking including two pots, plates, cups and a set of cutlery for each of them. Not exactly Dark Ages stuff, but his dad would pretend that they were, hoping to fire a desire in young Cade's heart for the past, but never really did. The Digital Age always won out, and his father would often concede, especially as his son got older. Camping out lost its flavor. Cade did not like the rain or the cold when in a tent, and the places they would visit would not have Wi-Fi or a mobile tower nearby to give him a connection to the internet. Cade also grew tired of the 'same old stories' his father would tell, what happened here or what happened there. Bryce was all too aware of Cade's growing disinterest and began telling fewer stories, and did not always take him along on his travels. Cade was growing up, able to look after himself more, he was not so dependent on dad. Just because this was right, it did not make it feel good. Yes, Bryce knew his son loved him, he also knew that Cade needed to make his own stamp on the world that he was discovering. He was a good lad, a sensible lad. Smart too. Bryce was all too proud of the young man Cade had become, he need not worry.

The car hit a pothole, "Everything's ok laddie, just a

small pothole that's all. These aren't the best of roads 'ere", the driver said. "You fell asleep, didn't wanna wake ya. We're not too far now. You hungry?" he continued.

"Er, no, but thanks. I'm good," replied Cade as he pulled the earbuds out of his ears, looking down at his Smartphone. He could not believe he fell asleep with the music still playing. The battery was almost dead, 'great!' thought Cade, 'just what I need', and was mad at himself.

"Here son, I got one of those thingy-ma-jiggy plug wires, charge 'er up." the driver said, reading Cade's face, as he handed over a car phone charger adapter. A little surprised, but relieved *and* grateful, Cade thanked the driver and plugged his phone in. Power!

"You're welcome, laddie. I got a son, uses that phone thingy all the time. Ain't got time for it meself, no. I'm kinda old-school, but my son got me this so we can stay in touch while I'm on the road. Can't get all those fancy things to work, don't understand 'em meself, but a phone's a phone and that's all I use it for. Not that it works a lot out 'ere, but I'm not this far out normally." Realizing what he just said, he ended with, "er, I'm sure it's 'cause I don't know what I'm doing".

They hit another pothole. "Better focus 'ere, laddie. Getting dark and all."

"Oh yeah, sure, and thanks again," Cade said.

He looked out the window, the sun was setting and the moon was starting to climb in the blanket of the growing night sky. He sat back and sighed. No city lights here, just the moon and stars that shone in between the cloud cover, as it revealed the starry hosts above. It was quiet, which was something Cade did miss. Nature's sound compared to none. Other than the sound of the engine, there was nature's stillness all about them.

Cade reflected on the past few weeks. Long journeys do that. It gives you time. And in that time he thought - a lot. He had been on the road for two days now. He could handle it, Cade was nearly seventeen and it was not the first time he had traveled alone, though admittedly it was the first time back to the UK by himself.

Bryce was invited to speak in a seminar at Whelhelm House University just outside of Seattle, Washington. The students and faculty loved the depth of knowledge that Bryce had so much, they asked if he could stay on for the rest of the semester. After the visas were granted, Bryce and his son Cade stayed on campus in the guest faculty wing. Cade was given the chance to enroll himself in some of the I.T. classes there too, while his student papers were transferred over to the university on a temporary education exchange program.   Here, Cade had the opportunity to further his studies in Science and Technology, which was not possible back in a Welsh/UK classroom. What started as a short-term stay, ended up being a long-term stay, over a year, in fact.

About two months into the second semester, a student in Professor Evans' seminar, (that's how they referred to him at the University), had found some information concerning a small town in the middle of Wales. A town called, Llandyke Wells. This, of course, got Professor Evans' attention. The student's name was a Carl McSmythe. He had brought in a somewhat peculiar stone that day. It was about the size of a goose egg, almost like a pebble, but not one naturally made by the rolling waves of the sea, this had been made by hand. The surface was somewhat smooth with irregular edges to it. Its color was ivory white. This was unlike any other stone, for when you tapped it on a hard surface it would send out something like a low audible resonating hum.

The stone was a gift to Carl when he was just a young boy, left to him by his late grandfather who received it from his great-grandfather generations ago. He used to tell a story of long ago, about a castle in Wales, England, and how, once upon a time, great wealth and power flowed in their family. Apparently, this stone was hewn from a rock found at the base of a tree and was meant to hold some mystical power. Engraved on one side of the stone was the symbol of a tree.

To a young boy, the magic and mystery of his grandfather's story ignited a great imagination. There was much more his grandfather shared, but as Carl grew older the memory of the story became more disjointed, merging with fairytales and books he had read. However, he always kept the stone safe for some reason and held on to it throughout all those childhood years, though somewhat forgotten.

The seminar lectures held by the Professor reminded Carl of that stone, so he went on a small treasure hunt of his own to dig it out from his dorm storage, to pay a little more attention to it. Vaguely remembering the story his grandfather told him, Carl did a little research for himself and found out that there was a Keep built on a hill in Llandyke Wells in Wales, called Byne Keep. The Keep was once part of Llandyke Castle built around 900 A.D., which was destroyed by fire only fifty years later. Only the Keep survived. A local Baron later occupied it and had the Keep reinforced with stone, and began to rule over the small nearby hamlets at that time. Upon further reading, he read about the usual folklore stories of the time. Tales of sorcery and battles between clans, treachery and plagues, mostly general stuff you would find commonplace during the Middle Ages. However, not much more was known, so Carl turned to his professor to see if he had any insight, since Professor Bryce was from Wales and may know more about the history of that time.

When Carl showed the stone to the Professor, his eyes widened a little, and his bushy eyebrows seemed to jump for joy, though he tried not to act too surprised by it. "So, where did you get this, son?" Bryce asked. Carl told him the story, which was even more intriguing to the Professor. "I see, I see", he replied, coolly as he rolled it around in his hand. "Well, yes I've seen similar stones like this before. It is a rune stone. Its size *is* a little unusual and the tree symbol is different, but I have seen rune stones with other etchings on them, but not quite like this. Byne Keep does have a lot of history surrounding it. I could look into it more." The Professor said, handing the stone back to Carl.

"No, no, you keep it. I don't think I can appreciate it the same way you can." Carl insisted, returning the stone to the Professor.

"Well, if you insist. But isn't it a family heirloom? How

about this, I'll keep a hold of it and see what I can find. And when I'm done, I'll return it to you." Bryce persisted.

"To be honest, I don't have much use for it, really. Forgot I even had it." replied Carl, "If it happens to hold an interesting story, maybe put it in a museum or something. Better than me using it as a paperweight", he jested.

The Professor smiled with a nod of his head and touched the rim of his hat in a kind of salute, while slipping the stone into his pocket.

"Oh, one more thing, Professor", Carl added, "Tap the stone on the table."

Professor Bryce looked a little puzzled. However, he took the stone from his pocket and tapped it on the table. "Well, would you look at that" he exclaimed a little surprised as the stone emitted a low hum.

"Weird, right! It's gotta be what - a kind of meteor stone or something, right?" quizzed Carl.

"Maybe, maybe" the professor replied slowly while stroking his black wispy beard.

"Well, see what you can find out, eh Professor?" said Carl

Looking down at the stone he slowly muttered, "Yes… yes", as his mind wandered for a moment. Professor Evans cleared his throat, then he looked back up at Carl. "Of course, …of course, sure. No problem," he smiled, "I'll find out what I can."

At the same time, when Professor Evans had tapped the stone on the table, across the other side of the campus, Cade was returning some books to the library, when he suddenly heard and *felt* a strange sound. It startled him so much that he let out a rather loud, "Whoah!", right there in the library, as he put his hand on his chest, buckling his legs and looking a little shocked. Those around him looked puzzled for his sudden outburst and started muttering to each other. Cade soon realized that no one else heard or felt what he just did. Being slightly embarrassed, he just smiled and shrugged. He finished returning the books to the librarian, who just looked at him with 'the look'.

A week later school was out for Spring Break, so Bryce took the opportunity to return to Wales, England, to check on some things. Cade stayed behind.

When school started back, Professor Evans had not returned. This was strange, Bryce was usually a punctual man, never really late for anything except when he was headlong into a relic hunting project. However, he had not had one for over a year now. The college expressed their concern. The students were missing class, which not a good thing. Calls were made but there was no answer. Cade started to worry a little. This had happened a few times before when his dad got involved in a project and forgot about the time, one of the few 'little' quirks his father had.

About two days into the semester, Cade received a telegram. Who sends telegrams in this day and age? he thought to himself, then he remembered - his grandfather would. The telegram said,

'Cade come home. Tickets and travel all arranged for you. Everything is fine. Your father needs you. Do not worry. Have sorted things out with the University. See you soon.'
- Grandpa

That was it. Cade did not know what to think. The Dean of the University said that the plane was scheduled to leave in a few hours and that he should pack as soon as possible. Cade packed a few of his things into a suitcase and his backpack, still a little bewildered, as he had no clue what was going on.

About an hour later, Cade was met again by the Dean,

"We'll give you and your dad some time, we can cover his base until you both return", he said, helping Cade to the cab that was waiting on the grounds, ready to take him to the airport.

"Oh, ok" Cade replied, "thank you, yeah, we'll be back soon."

He loaded his luggage into the cab and left the campus.

Thunder broke Cade's thoughts. The taxi was nearing the house of his grandfather, they were now on local roads, mud roads. Llandyke Wells in the rainy season was not a lot of fun when you're in the countryside. The driver honked the car horn a few times, "We're here, we're here, laddie. We made it. 'Ere lemme help you with your luggage."

The door to the cottage opened, it was grandpa Yates. Cade jumped out of the taxi as his grandpa came over to greet him, "Ahhhh, there he is! There he is!" he chuckled with his arms open wide. "Good to see you, sonny boy, been a while eh?"

They embraced each other. "Sure has, grandpa! Sure has." replied Cade.

"You boys get a move on, come inside, don't want you

both catchin' colds now." That was grandma standing in the doorway, "Come, come, say your hellos inside."

Grandpa Yates nodded to the taxi driver, thanked him and headed inside as the driver returned to his seat and drove back into town. It started to rain again.

Once inside, grandma Yates warmly hugged her grandson. "Look at you", she said softly with tears welling in her eyes, "My little Cade." She cupped his face gently with her hands as she looked up into his eyes, "Though not so little now, eh", she said with a smile, pinching his cheek. "Come, come, sit yerself down, sonny."

Tired from the long journey, Cade sat in a comfy chair. The cottage had not changed one bit from what Cade could remember, all those years ago when he was a young child.

"So then, where's dad?" asked Cade.

"Now sonny boy", his grandpa began, then changed direction a little, "ah look at you, a fine young man you turned out to be", he breathed, "Your father's fine, just fine son. Don't you worry. Right now, what you need is rest. Rest up, son. Ahh, you left a boy and returned a man. Good to see you, boy. Good, it is. No more talk tonight, get some sleep, we'll talk tomorrow."

As much as Cade wanted to know, somehow he was assured by his grandfather's words, after all, he *was* very tired, the journey had been long. Cade hugged his grandparents goodnight before he retired and went to his old room. He sat down on the bed and looked slowly around the room. Not one thing had changed, it was still the same room as when he was seven years old. He smiled and lay back on the bed as he tapped a toy plane on a string above his head, which made it swing back and forth. It did not take long before Cade fell right to sleep.

Chapter 2

❧ CADE ❧

It was the smell of bacon, sausages and eggs that woke Cade. It was 10:30 a.m. After he got himself together, he went downstairs. There on the table sat plates of Welsh bacon, sausages, poached eggs, laverbread and cockles, fried tomatoes and baked beans - all with a steaming pot of hot tea. He had not had laverbread in years. It was a true traditional Welsh delicacy. He remembered making it with his grandma when he was young. It's a dish that is made of seaweed and oatmeal. He would wait seemingly forever, as the seaweed was boiled on a low simmer for several hours until it became a thick puree. Next, came the messy part, they were shaped into patties then coated with oatmeal, before his grandma fried them in bacon fat. Fun memories.

"Ah, my boy! G'mornin'. Now sit yer'self down. Let's put some meat on those bones of yours." Grandma Yates said brightly. "Don't be shy, come now, dig in."

At that moment the side door opened, grandpa Yates walked in, "Don't think you're coming in with those boots on yer feet Kai," grandma Yates said.

"'Course not", grandpa quickly replied, looking over to Cade with a half-smile, "Ya see, son, that's a woman to love, right there. Knows just what to say."

Cade smiled. grandma Yates just exhaled, "Get on wit'yer," as she gave him a small kiss on the cheek.

"Makes it all worthwhile," he replied smittenly. "So son, you rested up? You slept half the morning," he teased, sitting himself down at the table. "Got a few things to do today, but we need to talk. And talk we will, after we eat. Come on, son, dig in, dig in."

Grandpa Yates motioned with his fork to Cade's plate. Grandma joined them, placing a stack of buttered toast on the table. "There now, let's eat," she said.

Cade looked over to his grandparents from across the table and smiled. His grandma had her grey white hair tied back into a bun, her skin was aged but still soft. When she smiled, her whole face lit up with a kind and loving glow that warmed hearts. Cade's thoughts flashed back to when he was a child. There he was, a boy of four years young, full of wonder and amazement. Before all the technology had invaded his world was a life of simple happiness.

Hard work, sweat, blisters and splinters used to be an everyday occurrence. He remembered sitting in this very room, in this very chair, barely able to see above the table. His grandma would get a cushion from the sofa for him to sit upon. Every time before they ate, he would stand on each chair around the table, and help set things up. He would put the knives, forks and spoons in their respective place around each empty plate. Sometimes he would climb up on the table, when his grandma was not looking, to place the cutlery down. He would always get found out because the knives and forks in some places would be set the wrong way around, with the knife and fork pointing towards the chair instead of away from it.

The smell of a lovingly cooked meal would come from the kitchen, to feed the hungry workers, - dad and grandpa. They would both come into the cottage with their muddy boots and grandma would fuss with them, not to bring them into the house. This always made young Cade smile.

This cottage was every bit a homely home, filled with knick-knacks from ages past, mostly local stuff. Things made by hand, and things brought from the marketplace or the local shops, were dotted along the mantelpiece over the fireplace. The walls held family photos and paintings by Welsh artists, portraying the rich green heritage of the Welsh countryside, valleys and hills. These paintings had darkened slightly with age. The gas light fixtures were still in their original place, though now had been converted over to electric light bulbs. The wooden floorboards had seen many days, were still strong but worn, and told a story all by themselves with scratches, dings and notches in them from past scrapes. On this floor sat the dining room table and chairs along with many other pieces of wooden furniture, all made by the hand of his grandpa, and some by his father. Those were good times, happy times.

It still had the same pleasant old cottage smell, another reminder of the past. Love and laughter sprinkled with a little sadness and a few tears, filled the nooks and crannies, making the home complete.

Seven years Cade had spent here. Seven years of adventure. Seven years of imagination. And now, he was back. Nothing seemed to have changed, except that everyone was a little older, and Cade himself a child no more.

Once the meal was over, Cade went to help do the

dishes, "No, no, son. But thank you. I got this now. You and your grandfather need to talk. Besides, there's that fence needs fixin' down yonder, and I'm sure grandpa could use a young strong arm like yours. Go on now," said his grandma.

"Better do as she says, son." grandpa interjected, "this is her domain, we got ours, come along now. I got some boots 'ere that'll fit you, those things on yer feet won't be looking the same after we're done. 'E 'ar son, put these on." He said, handing a pair of old boots to Cade.

"Thanks" Cade replied, taking off his trainers and putting the boots on. Once outside, grandpa Yates went over to the shed and pulled out some short planks of wood and a wooden post, along with a chainsaw, a shovel and a few other tools needed to fix the fence that was broken. Cade ran over to help him load them into a wheelbarrow.

"Aye, son! It's good to 'ave you 'ere," his grandpa said, "good, it is. 'Ere, you recognize this?" pointing to the wheelbarrow. "It's done me good now for nearly ten years. Come, look at the side 'ere".

At first, Cade was a little puzzled, then he saw it. Inscribed on the right side handle, notched by a small tool were the letters, C.A.D.E. His eyes widened, "wow", he said a little surprised, "I remember. You helped me build it."

"Now, now, son. I only helped with the lathe. You went an' cut the wood and hammered this together and sanded it down." grandpa Yates added. "aye, you were a quick learner. Good with your hands too. Still are, I'm sure. But we cannot stand around, gum yappin' about, we can talk as we walk, let's be goin'."

Up until this point, nothing was said about his dad's whereabouts, or why he was 'called' home. Not that he was worried. His grandfather's words put him at ease, knowing that, although *something* was going on, all was well. He found comfort being back. It was almost as if he was a child again, because nothing around him had changed at all. The village, the cottage, his grandmother, his grandfather, all set in the same motion of the past he knew. Cade smiled a little, put on some work gloves, picked up the handles of the wheelbarrow and followed his grandpa to fix the fence 'down yonder', however far that was.

About a half mile from the cottage, Cade and his grandfather stopped at a gate. They opened it, and walked into the field and closed the gate behind them. From here, you could see the downed fence across the other side of the field. A large tree branch had fallen on it, breaking the top two planks and the fence post had cracked under its weight.

The fallen branch would need to be cut into smaller pieces and the brush cleared away before it could be ready for them to repair what was damaged. His grandfather got right to work and cranked up the chainsaw. Cade dumped out the contents of the wheelbarrow, gathered the cut logs and started piling them into it. He did most of the lifting, although his grandfather could carry a weight himself, surprisingly easily. His grandfather was a few inches taller than Cade, his arms and legs were still strong and his frame stood firm. With both of them working together, it took a couple of hours to cut the branch into small logs and to clear the area. After a small break for lunch, they returned to work, setting the new post into the ground and replacing the damaged planks.

Cade wiped his forehead, he really enjoyed working with his grandpa again. It had been too long since the last time. This place held so many memories. Some good, some not-so-good. But this land was his home, his foundation, his heritage. His Welsh roots called to him from every direction. It was in every field, every tree, every cloud, it was in the breeze, in the chirping of the birds, everywhere, it surrounded him. An overwhelming experience surged through him. Cade sat on the wheelbarrow, soaking it all up.

"You ok, Cade?" said his grandfather, glancing towards his grandson.

"Yeah, I'm ok." Cade replied softly, looking down.

"It speaks to you, doesn't it? It's in yer blood, son. It's part of who you are. I know, I know." His grandpa said with his hands resting on top of the shovel, "I know that feeling meself. It's been a part of me for so long, can't imagine any place else." He paused as he looked slowly around, "You know son, your mother, my daughter, loved this place."

Cade could not believe his ears. His grandfather had never spoken about his mother before, and out of the blue like that, shocked him. "She helped me build this 'ere fence when she was 'bout your age." His grandfather continued, as he dug the shovel into the ground and tapped on the fence they just repaired. "A clever girl, quick-minded, and good spirited. Wanted to learn everything me and her mom did, and teach her we did.

"In fact, you remind us of her, there's a lot of your mother in you, Cade. You look a lot like her too, son." He paused, "I know... I know, we haven't spoken about your mother to you before. Guess you were a little too young to understand, and once you moved away an all, well, your father and I thought it best to wait. You had to find your own way. You know, forge your own path."

Cade was stunned and just sat there, absorbing the words of his grandfather.

"Just don't be upset, son. Maybe it was not the right thing, maybe it was. But we did what we did, thinking it was the best thing for you at the time." Grandpa Yates looked over towards Cade, "There's something about you, son, something deeper in you. It's in our bloodline, part of our heritage. It runs through your veins too. Your father doesn't 'ave what we 'ave. Sure, he's a great man, a good man, but he's only married into our family. It's the same for my dear sweet wife too, but you Cade, you are of my bloodline. You possess the inheritance of our ancestors. An inheritance you've not yet known, though it has always been there. You see, our roots go way back, further back than most. This 'ere land it holds many stories, secrets of old, legends even. Yep, there's many a folklore told about these parts, Cade, some of 'em true too."

His grandfather stood up and walked over to his grandson and looked him in the eyes, putting his hand on Cade's shoulder, "It ain't no accident you being here, Cade. You'll find out soon enough. In the days ahead, I will show you everything you need to know. No more secrets, no more mystery, just plain 'ol truth.

"There's destiny in you, Cade, you hear. It's the truth. And I believe that you're about to walk into that destiny." Taking the wheelbarrow in hand he said, "I know that this is a lot to take in right now, son. I'll give you time to digest what I'm saying. Don't you worry yerself, Cade. You have my word on it. I'll answer every question you may have. But for now, take what I've just said. Walk around a bit, I'll meet you back home. You know the way." And with that, he set on his way back towards the cottage.

Cade stood there for a moment. He was still. The words of his grandfather were still echoing all around him. In a half daze, he climbed over the fence they had just repaired and ventured down into the wooded area. 'Wow, that was a lot to take in', he thought. What it all meant, he really did not know, but something inside of him, something that was always there but had never surfaced, stirred in him. What that was, he could not tell either, but a calmness seemed to settle over him.

Leaning on a tree he looked up at the sky, watching the clouds drift by through the treetops above. He sighed. Looking back down again, he suddenly realized that he had been here before. Aside from a few bushes that had sprung up and a few young trees here and there, this was where he used to come when he was a child. He walked ahead and picked up speed as he moved along. An excitement rose within him. Careful not to trip on an exposed tree root, or bump into a low hanging branch, he ran towards an old memory. He stopped. There it was. He could not believe it, after all these years, withstanding the elements and time combined, stood his tree fort!

Young Cade, with his father, Bryce, and grandfather, Kai, built it together one summer for his sixth birthday. They spent weeks securing and rigging it together. Nails, screws, wood joints, ropes and pitch held it all together in place.

Cade just stood there, his eyes in wonderment, as if they were replaying the many scenes that took place there, all those years ago. He bent down, picked up a few small branches and stones on the ground and threw them up at the tree fort. He wanted to 'scare' any animal that may have taken up residence in it. He yelled a little as the branches hit the sides of the fort, but nothing moved or stirred.

To get into the fort, you had to climb up on the lowest branch, which then, was too high for young Cade, but easy for him now, so he went for it. He jumped up, grabbed on the branch, and pulled himself up. He climbed another, then another and reached his target. The fort was only built about eight feet off the ground, high enough for a young five-year-old, but low enough to withstand the elements, as the tree branches above became its natural canopy.

He tried the door. It did not budge. He tried again, nothing. The fort sure was sturdy, as it did not shake, creek or anything. Then he remembered, there was a secret way to unlock the door. His grandfather made it so that any wandering adventurer could not get in. You had to pull the door handle towards you, turn it to the right, push it back in then turn it to the left. Cade heard a small pop as the door opened. Cautiously he peered in, checking again for any intruders, but there were none. The tree fort seemed to take in a breath of fresh air, as he opened the door wider. It could not have been bigger than eight by six foot with a five and a half to six-foot high inclining ceiling. Small to Cade now, but plenty big for young Cade then.

Light poured in through the door revealing its contents. There was not much inside, just a few old wooden toys, a rug and a small bookshelf, which had a tin of crayons and pencils still in it, a table and a stool. In each corner of the fort was a wall mount, which housed a torch in each. Nailed to the wall were some hand-drawn pictures and there were some paper and old comic books on the floor, all of which had a coating of wood dust over it. It was musty inside, with that dry old aged wood smell, as it hadn't had fresh air moving within it for years. It still seemed just as strong, Cade hesitated, even though he was not so sure that he should go inside, he did.

Cade crossed his legs and sat inside the tree fort, he contemplated the day. He thought about his dad and wondered where he was, he thought about the words of his grandfather, he also thought about his mother. What was this about his bloodline and his heritage? What was his destiny? What did this all mean? What happened to his mother all those years ago? Why mention about her now? Where was his dad? Was there a common thread in it all? There were so many questions running through his mind, it was a little overwhelming.

All these questions cluttered his thoughts. Cade looked down, picked up one of the pieces of paper on the floor and glanced at it. It was a pencil drawing of a tree. He picked up another; again it was a line drawing of a tree. Looking at the other pieces of paper scattered about on the walls and floor, he noticed that they were all just drawings of what seemed like the same tree, apart from one. This one had other trees around it, all were colored in, the tree in the middle had been left blank, again, just an outline. 'That's strange', thought Cade, he did not remember having a love of trees, but it seemed like he did, with all these pictures he had drawn when he was a child. He put one of the drawings into his pocket, the rest he put down on the small table and went to leave. The sun was setting and it was beginning to get dark, he thought it was about time he had better head home.

Cade left the tree fort, locked it up again, climbed back down the tree and made his way back to the fence they had repaired earlier. As he strolled back, he thought again about the events of the day. It was a lot to take in, but for some reason Cade felt the emptiness that lay dormant inside him for years, begin to fill. It was like a kind of an awakening going on inside of him.

When he arrived back at the cottage, the sun had already set. His grandfather was outside locking up the shed for the night. "Evening son, you made it back, I see," his grandfather said.

"Sure did. Things haven't changed too much around here." Cade replied. "Hey, grandpa, guess what? I found the tree fort!" with a childlike excitement in his voice. "Oh, and I found this inside and many other drawings like it inside." Cade said, getting a piece of paper out of his pocket and handing it to his grandfather. "It seems like I loved trees when I was younger."

"Ah, yes son, the tree fort. I remember. Built to last that thing is." Replied his grandfather, as he took the piece of paper from Cade and looked at it. He paused. "Well, best be gettin' inside, rain's a-comin'," his grandfather responded.

After supper, Cade and his grandfather moved into the living room where a fire was slowly burning in the fireplace. "Ok. Now, son, I know you have questions, and like I said, I'll answer them all. But first, I got more to share with you." his grandfather said, as he opened up and placed the piece of paper Cade had handed to him earlier on the table.

"Thought you boys might like some refreshments before you get started", grandma interrupted, setting a tray of tea and biscuits on the coffee table.

"Now son," his grandfather continued, "Like I said, you have questions. And yes, I'll do my best to answer 'em. But first, let me finish what I started tellin' you. I think a lot of your questions will be answered in what I'm about to tell you."

CADE

Chapter 3

❧ THE TREE FORT ❧

C ade sat in the tree fort with his back against the wall and his feet crossed in front of him. He needed time to think, a place to get away from everything and sort out all the thoughts that were buzzing around his brain like busy bees. He did not get much sleep that night, he needed a place to unwind. And the tree fort was a perfect place.

In his childhood he had spent many a day here, and nights too. One adventure after another, he and his father would re-enact scenes they had read in books. It would be The Jolly Rodger sailing the seven seas, or it would be a castle, fending off the enemies from distant lands. Other times it would become a time machine and they would travel back in time to when dinosaurs roamed the earth, but today it was his think tank, a neutral zone.

A week ago, there he was, enjoying Spring Break while waiting for his dad to return from Wales, with not a care in the world. Only then to have his world turned upside down and to be catapulted back to Wales. If that was not bad enough, he then discovered that all that he had previously known, was not really quite the way it was. Not that that was bad, just amazingly more interesting. This whole whirlwind course of events was a lot to digest, but strangely started to make sense to him, the more he thought about it.

Cade recounted the words his grandfather spoke the night before. It sounded quite unbelievable, but the more he spoke, the more the words came alive. The picture he painted was so surreal, that it was hard to believe that it was really true. It was almost like something you would read in a book or watch in a movie, a fantasy even, but this was different. This was real. With every word his grandfather spoke, something inside of Cade connected itself to those words. Unknowingly, Cade was an intricate part of the tapestry that was being woven right before his eyes. The baton, as it were, was being passed from grandfather to grandson. What now lay before Cade was a mission that encompassed his past and his present, his ancestry and his heritage. As Cade sat there, listening, it was as if all the pieces fitted together, and all the questions he had were answered. When his grandfather had finished speaking, he made a request to Cade. "So son, are you ready to face the uncertain? Are you prepared to carry the family legacy and walk down our ancestral path, for the greater good? You now are their only hope, what are you going to do?"

Cade reached into his backpack and pulled out a sandwich that his grandmother had made. She insisted that he should take some food with him, in case he stayed out a while. They knew he needed time alone, so they gave him that. Cade sure had a lot to think about, but being the kind of lad he was, they felt confident that he could handle it. He bit into the sandwich, looking out of a small window of the tree fort. It had started to rain. He took another bite. "This kinda thing is only supposed to happen in the movies." he said to himself as he sat back down. "Only thing is, this ain't no movie".

As the rain fell on the leaves of the trees above, Cade picked up one of the papers with a tree he had drawn on it, when he was younger, from the small table next to him. He stared at it. The longer he looked at it, the more his grandfather's words came to life. Cade could actually hear his grandfather share the story of his ancestry, awakening his very soul.

"Cade, our family has been around for many, many years. Down through the ages, we have kept a secret. This secret was kept, even from you, for your protection; not that you were or are in harm's way. But when your mother disappeared, your father and I thought it best that we didn't raise you with this burden. You had to find your own path and discover your own passions in life to live by.

"You have become a very focused young man. Sensible, mature and an innate ability to see things differently and know how things work, even without much study or guidance. Though you did not know it, these are just some of the gifts that you possess. You are your mother's child, my grandson. You stand on the edge of our ancestry. You have inherited a history far bigger than all of us, and your role in all this has only just begun. Heed these words, young Cade, and fear not. All the tales, the folklore and the mysteries are about to unfold right before you. Drink your tea, it's gonna be a long night."

Thunder rolled across the sky as the rain fell heavier. Cade finished his sandwich as he looked out of the window again. It looked like he was going to have to stay here until the storm passed, however long that was going to be. Cade was glad that he had shelter, the tree fort sure was built to withstand the elements. He sat back down, reached into his backpack and retrieved his Smartphone. He checked for a signal; nothing. "Just great!" Cade muttered to himself. He tapped the screen to find his music folder on the SD card, put the earbuds in his ears and tapped on the music player.

He needed to relax and take his mind off things, even if it was just for a moment. Cade rested with his hands behind his head on the backpack and closed his eyes. Shortly after, he fell asleep.

"Cade. Cade!" a voice called out. "Cade. Are you in there?" the voice said again. There was a knocking on the door. "Hello, hello, Cade." the voice persisted.

Cade sat up, pulled the earbuds out of his ears and rubbed his eyes. "Huh" he said, "who...who's there?" he asked in half a daze, yawning.

"Cade, I need your help, please...let me in", the voice asked; it sounded like a woman's voice.

"Who is it? Who are you? What's the matter? How do

you know my name?" Cade replied as he cautiously edged towards the door on his knees and looked through a small hole. He could not see anyone.

"Cade, please, just open the door. I'm...I'm your mother.", the voice said.

Stunned, Cade, mouthed the words, 'my...my mother', 'impossible'. His voice started to shake, "n...no. I-I-It can't be!" He backed away.

"Open the door, Cade. Please, I need your help, we need to rescue your father.", the voice insisted back.

Suddenly a loud clap of thunder roared across the sky as a bolt of lightning struck the trees above. The sound of a big crack followed and a large tree branch fell from above. It landed on the tree fort, jolting it from its secured position. it did not fall, just tilted a little. Rainwater began to trickle through the breach in the roof that poured down soaking Cade. He woke from his sleep, as he pulled the earbuds out of his ears. Startled, he stood up quickly, bumping his head on the ceiling. Pain followed as he clutched the top of his head, his heart was racing. The rain was still pouring into the fort, he had to leave, even though his head was stinging. A little dazed, he crawled over to the door and went to open it. He withdrew his hand, remembering 'the voice' behind the door. He took a deep breath and opened it. No one was there. He looked down, no one, nothing. His head started to pound. Climbing down, careful not to slip on the wet branches, he made it to the ground.

He looked up to survey the damage. A thick, heavy branch had fallen through the tree fort, dislodging it from its original position. His eyes searched for 'the voice' high and low, he looked all around, but no one was there, he was alone. He checked to see how badly he had knocked his head, with his fingers. He winced as he touched a small open cut. Cade tucked his sleeve cuff into his hand and pressed down against the wound.

He was mad at himself. The storm above showed no sign of stopping anytime soon, so Cade decided to head back home. Another clap of thunder rolled across the skies, followed by a flash of lightning as the wind blew strong. Cade ducked down, things were beginning to look a little dangerous. Small branches and leaves whirled around him. An old half-dead tree, not more than ten yards away started to creak, as it swayed back and forth, popping as it went. He ran as fast as he could to get out of the woods, being here in a storm was not safe. The ground was wet and muddy, making it difficult to run without slipping, especially with one hand on top of your head. He heard a loud snap, snap, snap as the half-dead tree fell then finally rested on the ground, missing him by inches. Cade lost his footing and tumbled forward. Fortunately, he reached a clearing in the woods, wet, muddy and in pain. He sat for a moment to catch his breath. He checked the top of his head, at least it had stopped bleeding.

He could not believe what had just happened. It was too much. Cade let out a loud cry. He was mad. Mad at everything. He thumped the ground a few times as muddy water splashed up on his face. "Great!" he said loudly, "just great!"

He stood up, shook his arms and wiped his forehead with his wet sleeve. "Ok, Cade. You got this. You're ok. Just a little wet." he said to himself, shaking his arms again. He could not get any wetter than he was. A little disoriented, Cade looked around to get his bearings and began to make his way back, though he was not really sure where he was. He had to find shelter, somewhere. He looked over across the clearing and saw what looked like some rocks, so he headed in that direction. Sure enough, they were rocks, jutting out from the ground forming a kind of natural canopy on the hillside there. He sheltered himself under them. Not the most comfortable place, but at least it was dry and kept the wind and rain from soaking him further.

'Some day *this* is turning out to be', he thought to himself, as he looked at his surroundings. He noticed that these rocks went a little further back, into a small cavern-like area, so he cautiously ventured inside. It was empty. Abandoned by whatever used to shelter here before, leaving nothing but dried leaves, twigs and a few broken branches. He gathered them together and thought about building a small fire. It was not safe to start one inside, so he checked outside to see if there was a dry enough place to set one up. He found a ditch surrounded by a small circle of stones, away from the entrance, to the right. Someone had obviously been here before and used it as a shelter at some point, and this was the fire pit.

He gathered the kindling together, remembering his camping days with his dad, picked up two flint-like stones that were scattered here and there, and promptly started a small fire. 'A break! Just what I need' he thought to himself. Though he was never a cub scout, Cade's father taught him how to 'live-off-the-land' so to speak. Something Cade was grateful for, especially now. Cade sat on a rock looking at the fire dancing around as it crackled and popped. The storm had calmed down a little, with the rumbles of thunder off in the distance, though the rain still came.

Watching the fire as it burned, he was taken back to a similar fire that burned in the fireplace of his grandparents' cottage the night before.

"Your father was on a mission" his grandfather continued. "Ever since his wife disappeared fourteen years ago, he willed himself to find her. I, at first, attempted to help, being her father, but found age had got the better of me, I just could not do it. I was powerless to bring her back. Therefore, your father took the quest. The task he was about to undertake was a dangerous one but it was the only hope we had.

"You see, Cade, as you know, my name is Kai, though I have not always gone by that name; I was known as 'the Keeper'. I hold the keys to the doorway into the past. Now these are not physical keys, no, no. The keys are in my voice. I am able to lock and unlock the door that leads to certain points in time in the past. I taught this ability to your mother, my daughter, Maelona. It was my duty to pass along the legacy of our ancestry."

Tears began to well up in his eyes, "Ah yes, a beautiful young girl. Maelona was our star, full of talent, full of life. She grew and wielded her abilities far beyond that of my own. Then one day, she found her love, your father, Bryce. They married and Bryce became family. Bryce soon learned our ways and embraced our history, even though he himself could not enter through the doorway, he was encompassed in the lifeline of our heritage. "

"A few years later, you were born.   And what a wonderful time that was. You were the greatest thing she ever accomplished. She used to dance around the house with you when you were just a babe in arms. You truly were the joy of your mother and father's heart."

"When you were about a year and a half old, she wanted to take you to the door. Maelona wanted to teach you the ways of our ancestors, as I did with her. With my guidance, Maelona would take you along with her as you would both pass through the doorway only to return moments later back to our time. This went on for several months. Each time, you both stayed a little longer. Then one day..." his voice trailed off. Grandma reached over and touched his hand, "then one day, only you returned. I did not know what to think. Nothing like this ever happened before. I tried every way I could to bring her back but each time I opened a door, she was not there. She just was not there.   I exhausted myself, door after door, nothing, nothing, nothing. Afraid I was about to collapse the portal,

I closed every door. Shut them tight, until the time came for us to bring her back.

"Maelona was smart. She knew. She knew that we would find a way, so much so that she herself had left us a key, the only one of its kind. She had hidden it, wrapped up in your blanket and tied around your chest. It was the Celtic Oval."

Finally, the storm had passed. The small fire Cade had built did its job. At least he was dryer now. He stomped out the remaining burning embers and headed back, as best as he could recollect, towards the tree fort. He had about two hours left of daylight, and he figured he was about an hour away from the cottage. 'What a difference it makes when it's not raining,' Cade thought. Trekking back was easier and soon he found his way back again, past the fallen tree and to his childhood tree fort. The weight of the branch that had fallen on it caused the branches beneath to sag a little. It was still very secure as far as he could see, so he climbed up and entered the tree fort to retrieve his backpack. The shift caused everything to tumble down to one side. Leaves, paper and pieces of small branches were everywhere; the hole in the roof did not help. But he was sure he and his grandfather could fix the damage. He picked up his backpack. It was dripping wet. There on the floor was his Smartphone with earbuds attached, "Aw man" Cade said, sounding annoyed. "just great!". It was lying in a pool of water. He picked it up and water poured from its insides, he wrapped the ears buds around the phone and put it in his pocket. "That ain't gonna work again", he said in an unhappy tone. He left the tree fort and headed back to the cottage.

THE TREE FORT

Chapter 4

❧ MAEL ❧

Cade was lying on his bed looking up at the ceiling while examining his Smartphone. Not only had it been soaked with water but there was a crack running across the screen. He opened the back and pulled the mini SD Card out, hoping that the data on it was not damaged in any way. Cade tossed the Smartphone onto the table next to the bed, turned his head and looked out of the window, tucking his hands behind his head. Grandma had cleaned the wound on the top of his head whilst he told them what happened earlier. Fortunately, it was a small cut, nothing serious, though it still felt tender. The moon shone brightly through the window. It was a clear and cloudless night. Cade got up and walked over to the window and looked out. Everything looked a silvery blue. All was still. His eyes scanned the landscape. Over in the distance was Glynn Hill, he could see the ruin of Byne Keep. It stood there cold and broken in the light of the moon. Something caught his eye. It seemed like he could see a light or something, maybe a reflection from inside the Keep. As soon as he noticed it, it disappeared. He shrugged, dismissing what he had just seen, or may have seen. "What a day", he said quietly to himself, as he returned to his bed, resuming his position.

The voice he heard when he was in the tree fort earlier haunted him. Though he knew it was a dream, it seemed so real, like he had really heard it. Cade took a deep breath and closed his eyes. That voice, the woman's voice, his *mother's* voice, echoed in his ears. "Could all this be true?" he muttered to himself. A small tear ran from the corner of his eye and down the side of his face. The grandfather clock downstairs sounded its hourly chimes, breaking the silence. With each chime, Cade's grandfather's words cut through into his thoughts.

"Ah yes, the Celtic Oval, it was a powerful device, *is* a powerful device, made and crafted so many centuries ago.

It had long been lost and forsaken, thought never to be seen again. But, somehow, my daughter had found it, and sent it back with you, to your father and I. Something had happened, what we did not know, but this was a sure sign that things were about to change. The only way we could help, even if we could, would be because of the Celtic Oval.

"Now Cade, to understand about the Oval, you first have to understand its origin, where it came from, who made it, and why. But I guess to answer those questions, I have to go further back in time to where it all began.

These doorways to the past I've been talking about, young Cade, are found in this tree. Oh, not just any tree, no, no, not by any means, it's what we refer to as The White Tree, the only one of its kind. Its origin goes back over a thousand years, during the dawn of the Dark Ages. The White Tree is a tree of power, made almost solely out of pure energy. It was born out of a tear from the dying wife of a alchemist named Mael.

Mael and his wife were, in fact, both Alchemists, well-practiced in the art of science, philosophy and mysticism, using their abilities for good, whenever and wherever they could. They married young and were very much in love. The two were inseparable, never far from each other's side. They both had a love for nature, animals, birds and land alike. Always helping and healing wounded creatures of the forest by using their abilities.

Back then, the practice of alchemy was something people were superstitious about, and many townsfolk shunned such people and would often keep their distance. However, Mael and his wife were different, never to be feared for their abilities but rather, welcomed. Still they never made it known publicly to those around them, for there were those who practiced evil, and the darkness of the art causing harm to others, and used their ability to promote themselves for fame and fortune.

In their travels around different parts of Wales, they came upon the land of Llandyke Wells and settled here, making it their home. Mael was strong and being good with his hands, built a small home for them both to live in. Together with his wife he began to seed and plant the land to provide food for them.

In the years that followed, they decided it was time to start a family, but sadly came to realize that this was not possible. Years had passed, some twenty years or so, and still they were without children. Then a plague swept through the land, where many people died. Being so far away from the nearest town and townsfolk, Mael and his wife thought that they were safe from the plague ever reaching them. However, one day, Mael's wife was out in the woods collecting some wild mushrooms when, all of a sudden, she accidentally disturbed a small rat's nest. In the fray, one of the rats scratched her. In fear, she ran as best she could back to her home and called for Mael. The Alchemist used his healing ability to mend and restore the small puncture in her ankle, never noticing the small red flea bites above her ankle. All was well for a day or so until his wife started becoming really sick; a blackness had crept up from where these fleas had bitten her. Her breath became shallow and the color of her skin had turned a ghostly grey. The plague had its grip on her. There was little time left, she was dying. Mael's only hope now was to take her to the Rock of the Celt, the name given to a mystical stone that lay in the ground, white with age where lightning had struck it so many times.

As the story goes, Mael carried his wife over to this Rock and placed a tear from his dying wife on it. He uttered a few words and lifted his hands. The sky above turned dark as billowing clouds formed up above, a bolt of lightning struck the teardrop for what seemed like several seconds. What happened next had never happened before. In an instant, a young shoot began to grow out from the rock where the tear lay. The small shoot grew big and strong, right before their eyes. The Rock of the Celt split, cracked, and split again, as the shoot twisted and turned, as it grew upward, forming itself into a leafless tree, tall and white. A burst of energy then surged from within the tree, sending a shock wave that went through Mael and his dying wife, knocking them both to the ground. Moments later Mael arose and there he saw his wife, she was standing by the tree, bright with life, sickness free, with a new glow upon her countenance. Mael himself had changed too, he felt strong again, like life itself had breathed upon every cell of his body and regenerated his being. He walked over to his wife and held her hand, both overjoyed at this new lease of life that they had been given.

Mael reached out to touch the White Tree. As he did so, a portal opened on the wall of the trunk and they stepped inside. Suddenly they were caught up in the heart of the tree, as their feet left the ground, they spun slowly around. Something like white liquid fire blazed all around them, flashing scenes from the outside before their eyes. At first, they did not know what to make of it, but then they realized what they were seeing. They saw the future, the past and the present. They saw realms and kingdoms rise and fall. It seemed like an eternity but also as a moment, as scene after scene flashed before their eyes. With each scene, words appeared before them in a language they had never seen before, but somehow knew. And as soon as it happened, it stopped and they found themselves standing outside at the base of the tree once again.

For the next sixty years, Mael and his wife learned more about the White Tree and the power it possessed. During those sixty years, they never aged much at all. The White Tree had not only healed his wife from the plague but had somehow also infused them with age defying longevity. Not only that, but much to their surprise and joy, Mael and his wife were with child, even though by now they had to have been nearly ninety years old. When the time had come for the baby to be born, they found that they were not blessed with just one child, but three. Triplets! The first two were born quickly, a boy and a girl, but the third child took its time. Two days had passed before the third was born, taking a great toll on Mael's wife. So much so that his wife's strength had weakened so much, that she could barely breathe. Two boys and one girl. The first two were born strong and healthy, but the third was born small and weak. Not knowing quite what to do, Mael's wife told him to take the baby to the tree and maybe it would heal the child like it did her many years ago. So that's what Mael did. When he reached the White Tree he opened the portal, stepped inside, laid the baby in the center of the floor and put his hands on the baby. A jolt of energy from the heart of the tree surged through the baby's frail body, just like Mael remembered all those years ago when the Tree first appeared before them, healing his wife and giving new life to his own body.

A small cry came from the baby as color flashed across his body. The baby was made well, looking as strong and healthy as his two other siblings. In great delight, Mael took the baby in his arms and ran home to his wife. However, she seemed no better but was glad to see her third born well.

During the next few days, his wife was not getting any stronger, so Mael gathered his children and wife together and made his way back to the White Tree. He opened the portal, carried his wife inside and laid her gently on the floor. Mael looked up into the heart of the tree with tears in his eyes, as he cried out. His wife took his hand and stroked his head, then held his face in her hands, wiping his tears with her thumb and said softly, "It's ok, it's going to be ok. Look after them for me." He looked into her eyes with pain etched across his face, she seemed at peace as she smiled softly, "Mael, you're going to be just fine, you'll be a great father, raise them well. I love you." With that, she laid back down and her body went limp.

Everything around Mael suddenly began to shake, as a burst of light shone bright all about. A peace began to settle upon Mael's heart, then, as the light faded, the body of his wife was gone. In her place lay a small ivory-white stone, no bigger than a goose's egg. Etched upon that stone was the symbol of the Tree. Mael just sat there, alone, his eyes fixed on the stone. The cry of the babies outside broke the silence, "Go Mael", the voice of his wife softly echoed around him, "they need you now. Take the stone, I will always be with you."

His grandpa sat back in his chair and rubbed the sides of his face and interlocked his fingers together, resting them on his chest. His eyes were etched with years past, yet they looked youthful as he unraveled the history of their family ancestors. "Aye, and for the next forty-odd years, Mael raised his three children as best he could, teaching and training the triplets to live off the land, while they discovered their own gifts, strengths, and abilities.

"Ardwyadd, he was the firstborn. His strength was

unmatched, even wrestled with a bear once, leaving without even having a scratch on him. He became a skillful hunter in bow, spear and slingshot. Next in line was Iola, his daughter. She inherited many of her mother's attributes. Her gift enabled her to grow almost anything, in any type of soil and it would flourish; even dying and dead plants would regenerate and become healthy again. Then there was Cadarn. He was sharp-minded and energetic, quick to learn and skilled himself in wood, stone and metals.

"All three children, just like their father, looked far younger than they should have done. It seemed that they too had inherited this age-defying gene, although being the same age, Cadarn looked the youngest out of the three.

"Not only did Cadarn look younger, he was also more inquisitive and daring, always pushing things to the limit. From a very young age, he spent a lot more time in the White Tree than his brother and sister did. His connection with the Tree was different too, it was somewhat stronger than even that of his father. Cadarn sought to learn and discover all he could, even secrets that his own father, Mael, never knew. Then one day, there *was* a discovery that he made, one that changed everything."

Chapter 5

❧ THE CELTIC OVAL ❧

It was late and Cade could not sleep. He went downstairs to make a cup of tea, being careful not to wake his grandparents. As the kettle boiled, Cade leaned back on the kitchen counter and looked into the room. It sure was surreal being back here again, reminiscing childhood memories, and hearing stories about it, as his eyes danced around the kitchen. How much simpler things were back then.

The water boiled, Cade brewed himself a cup of tea and sat at the kitchen table. He sat there for a while just looking at the cup of hot tea as the steam from the water spiraled gently into the air, reminding him of the tea his grandma made, not more than twenty-four hours ago.

"Makes a great cuppa tea, don't she son?", his grandpa said as he took a sip of tea. "Just what you need, whet the ol' throat, you know. Ok, now where was I?" He paused, "Ah yes. Cadarn!"

"One night, after his father, brother, and sister left the White Tree to return home, Cadarn stayed behind for a while, as he often did.

After a short time later this particular night, Cadarn thought he smelled fire. Then he heard fire, it came out of nowhere. Suddenly he found himself engulfed in a blaze of fire that surrounded him. There was no way out. In a panic, Cadarn fell to the floor and covered himself with his cloak. His heart was racing, not fully knowing how to escape. Then he realized that he felt no heat. He looked out from under his cloak and saw the blazing fire all around him, but the flames did not harm him. He reached out to touch the flames, nothing! Not even a burn. Then he heard a scream behind him, he turned and saw a young woman, trapped in a barn that was ablaze. She had taken refuge in a horse trough filled with water, trying to escape the flames. She reached out to him for help. Cadarn got up and held on to her hand to pull her to safety, but when he pulled her towards himself, he found that she could not enter into the safety of the White Tree. He tried again, but it seemed like an invisible force field stopped her from entering. Again he tried, again she could not enter.

Then all of a sudden, the scene before him disappeared and a woman's soft gentle voice echoed around him.

'She cannot come with you, but save her you can.
Seek into the Tree and the Rock where you stand.
For in it you find your Lifestone, one apiece.
United together, tree and stone, bring release.'

"Cadarn was once again alone in the Tree, bewildered at what just took place. Questions filled his mind. 'Who was that girl caught in the midst of the fire and HOW could she see him inside the Tree? Whose voice was that?' Determined to find the answers, Cadarn's curious nature drove him to find a way to save the young girl he had seen in the vision. Who she was, he did not know, but something inside him knew that she could be rescued from that barn fire somehow. The one thing he did know was that she was very beautiful. All this he kept to himself. When he arrived home, Cadarn did not tell anyone, not even his father. He then sought a way to bring her through the portal."

"For the next few days, Cadarn was unusually quiet, which then raised a little concern that something was not right. Mael asked his son what was troubling him, but Cadarn just shrugged it off, saying all was well. But Mael knew otherwise.

"One night, shortly after he had his vision in the White Tree, Cadarn had a dream. In the dream, he saw the White Tree with its energy flowing inside it. He saw this energy, like the sap of a tree, being fashioned by hand into an ornate oval shaped object. Five stones appeared and embedded themselves into it. Upon its completion, a burst of power pulsed out from within the ornate oval. It was then placed in the hands of another, enabling them to enter and travel through the portal of the White Tree.

"The next thing he saw was a blackened billowing cloud creeping over the oval, and a tempest storm swirled around it gaining in power and strength. The light that surrounded the oval began to grow dim as the billowing clouds completely engulfed the oval. A loud rumbling sound came from within the midst of it all, followed by a loud explosion. The dark storm clouds were no match for the brilliance of light that shone out from the oval. However, in the fray of it all, the oval shattered into pieces and the embedded stones were thrown in every direction, each one lost within its own space and time. The shattered oval pieces began to fall like snow, covering the surrounding land. These fragments then pooled themselves together, into something like a mystical glittering stream, which flowed towards the White Tree. Up and around the trunk it swirled, entwining around each branch and limb, like a small vine climbing up a beanpole. A burst of dazzling light suddenly shone from within the heart of the White Tree as it began to sparkle all over. The fragments then gently rested upon the limbs of the tree. For the first time ever, the White Tree bloomed with a star bright array of glistening white blossom."

"Early the next morning, Cadarn, armed with the voice, the vision and now the dream, made his way quickly to the White Tree. Once there, he knelt down at the white rock beneath the Tree and touched it and uttered the words '*Rhydd Fy Carreg Mywyd*', which means, 'Free my Lifestone'. A light began to glow from under his hand, which was followed by a cracking and splitting sound as a small egg-shaped stone fell into his hand. Cupping this stone in his hands, Cadarn gently blew away the rock dust that covered its surface, as a small rune symbol burned into it. The symbol consisted of three lines, the two outer lines curved to the left and right, while the middle line was straight.

"What are you doing!?", came the stern voice of his father behind him. Mael was not happy, "What have you done!? Do you have any idea what you are getting us all into?" he continued taking a hold of Cadarn's arm.

"But Father..." Cadarn replied

Mael interrupted, "NO! This is wrong, I cannot allow you to contin..."

"I'VE GOT TO SAVE HER!" Cadarn yelled out. "She needs my help." Tears were welling up in his eyes, "I can't explain it, but I have just got to save her. She'll die if I don't." he continued. "I...I had this vision a few nights ago, here...right here in the Tree," pointing to the White Tree. "A girl was trapped, surrounded by fire and I could not save her. I tried but she could not come into the Tree, it kept pushing her back...."

"Cadarn", Mael said softly, "You know that's impossible, no one outside of our bloodline can enter, I thought you knew that? Listen, son, this isn't the answer"

"YES, yes it is." He snapped back, "You don't understand! The voice in the Tree told me!"

"The voice in the Tre..." Mael repeated, and then he trailed off. He was taken off guard a bit as he stumbled back, looking up at the White Tree. "A voice", he said clearing his throat, "A voice, you say?"

"Father, please...", Cadarn started to say.

Mael motioned with his hand, "Now hold on there, son." He was looking up at the White Tree, his eyes remembering a past comfort. "A voice, yes... yes. The voice of my sweet dear wife, no doubt. The voice of your mother." he said with a half-smile. "Hmmm," he said as he looked down shaking his head a little, closing his eyes.

"Cadarn, I know.", Mael said compassionately, putting his hand on his son's shoulder. "Yes, I know what's been troubling you these past few days, son. Don't you forget now; I know this Tree very well. I've seen things from the past and things from days to come. What once was the future has become today, and I've got to accept that." He paused.

"I know about the dream you had, last night son. I saw it too! Aye now, don't be too surprised, the White Tree connects us in ways that are still a mystery. But, I must caution you, Cadarn. The latter of what you saw in the dream, brings trouble. This oval object comes with a cost. Our Lifestones, and our connection with the Tree, are all linked together, and if anything should happen, who knows what the consequences could be.

"Save the girl, you must. Just understand this one thing,

Cadarn, be prepared to embrace all that is to come as a result of what you are about to do."

At that moment, Cadarn's brother, Ardwyadd and his sister, Iola both came towards them.

"So, a bunch of early birds, eh?", Ardwyadd teased. "Come on now, work to be done"

"Ardwyadd," Iola interjected, "Can't you see that father and Cadarn were talking about a serious matter." Being perceptive, she continued, "Yes...yes, it concerns us all. We...we have to save a girl."

Ardwyadd looked puzzled. Cadarn and his father looked at each other. Mael just smiled a little and mouthed the words "We're connected."

"Her name is Seren, ...yes, that's her name. You need our Lifestones to save her - come we don't have much time," she said with some urgency.

She bent down, placed her hand on the Rock and whispered the words, *'Rhydd Fy Carreg Mywyd'*. Like before, a light began to glow from under her hand, followed by a cracking and splitting of rock as a small egg- shaped stone fell into her hand. As she blew on the stone a symbol of a leaf burned itself into it.

Ardwyadd followed suit and did the same. As he blew the dust off his stone, the symbol of a bear was revealed.

Last was Mael. He looked up at the Tree and knelt down, placing his hand on the Rock. When he spoke the words, the whole place shook. A great cracking and splitting of stone rumbled from deep within the Rock itself, the ground shuddered almost knocking everyone off their feet. Then there was silence. Mael held in his hand his Lifestone, it was about the size of a small goose egg, and just like the others, he blew off the dust. As he did so, a symbol of a rock burned itself into its surface.

"Ok, let's go, into the Tree. We've got work to do." Ardwyadd said. That made everyone else look at each other in surprise. Mael smiled, "Ha, ha!" he laughed as he patted Ardwyadd's broad shoulder, "Indeed, my boy, let's go."

Once inside the White Tree, Mael, Ardwyadd, Iola and Cadarn stood in a circle and lifted their hands. Using all their abilities together, the sap of the White Tree swirled around them. Round and round it swirled, as the four slowly fashioned the sap from the Tree into an ornate Celtic Oval. The four Lifestones was placed into the Oval. Mael had a small leather bag that was tied with string, which he had kept around his neck for the past forty-plus years, which he now took off. Inside the bag was a stone, similar to his own, except the symbol on this stone was a tree.

"This, my children, is your mother's Lifestone", Mael

said, solemnly, "It completes the circle."

As soon as the last Lifestone was placed in the Celtic Oval, something like lightning coursed through it, making the whole oval shrink in size.

Cadarn took a hold of the Celtic Oval and as he did so, fire engulfed them. The girl screamed out, just like before. Mael, Ardwyadd, and Iola were taken aback at the scene.

"It's ok everybody, the fire is not going to hurt us here." Cadarn called out above the roar of the fire. "Ardwyadd, I'm going to need your help."

Wooden beams were falling as the fire spread rampantly throughout the barn. Ardwyadd and Cadarn entered the burning shelter as wood embers fell around them. The smoke was getting thicker, making it hard to breathe. Then the roof of the barn started to give way, creaking and cracking under the weight, as the lower structure was robbed of its strength and the fire raged its destruction.

The main beam of the roof started to collapse. Ardwyadd ran over to the beam and held it up.

"Grab the girl," he yelled out, "I've got this," as his muscles strained, preventing the beam from falling on top of the girl.

Cadarn ran over to the girl who was watching from the

horse trough. He picked her up as he made his way back to the Tree.

"Here, take a hold of this." Cadarn told the girl.

The young girl did as she was told and was able to enter into the White Tree. Once inside they heard a loud crash behind them. The barn had collapsed in on itself. Fire, embers, and smoke rolled across the floor like a wave crashing upon a shore.

"ARDWYADD!!" Cadarn cried out.

The fire raged.

"Ardwyadd…." He repeated, falling to his knees in grief.

Then, bursting out from the flames, he came. Running towards the White Tree and made it safely inside."

Grandpa Kai repositioned himself in his chair, as he continued. "Soon after the rescue of the girl, Mael doubled up his effort to plant even more trees. Throughout the years he had seeded acres of woodland which eventually turned to the forest you see today. Mael wanted to 'hide' the White Tree, for he feared now that since the creation of the Celtic Oval, unwanted and power-hungry persons would want to seize it and utilize the White Tree for themselves. His foresight was not wrong."

THE CELTIC OVAL

Chapter 6

❧ BYNE KEEP ❧

Cade was up early the following morning, shoved some laverbread and a packet of biscuits into his backpack and ran out the door. Something that caught his eye last night was playing on his mind, and he had to investigate.

It was quite a hike, several miles in fact, but Cade made the trip. A couple of hours later, he arrived at his destination, Byne Keep. There it stood, thick black blocks of stone, towering above. Claimed only by the wildlife and the vegetation that now resided there, owned by no one, or so it seemed.

Cade rested on one of the stones there, as he looked out over Glynn Hill. The green heads of the forested woodlands blanketed the countryside, in between pockets of grassy fields and farmlands. "These trees" he muttered to himself, as his thoughts wandered back...

"Yep," his grandpa continued, "that was the beginning of a whole lot of change! You see, the creation of the Celtic Oval, never really sat too well with Mael. For he feared that once in the wrong hands, the power of the White Tree would be exploited, leading to disastrous consequences. So, he set a guardian over it. Ardwyadd to be exact. After all, he was the eldest and strongest. The Celtic Oval was to be kept inside the safety of the White Tree at all times, until it was needed and therefore, one of only four people could access it. And hence, Ardwyadd became the Keeper of the Tree.

"Now, Mael was not too fond of change, but of course had to accept it, as time went on. Cadarn was the first to get married. Seren, the girl he rescued, became his bride and became part of the family. As it turned out, she too became somewhat connected to the life of the White Tree, as our longevity and slow aging was transferred over to her too. New secrets were beginning to unfold, and, as the years rolled by, Mael started to get more and more concerned. As a result, he continued planting even more trees. Soon the woodlands turned into forest that stretched on for miles all around where the White Tree stood.

"Now there was a wealthy and powerful man who came down from the north, Arthus of Smythe, who took possession of the Keep upon Glynn Hill. No one stood in opposition at the time, until one day a decree went out, which demanded all the local townsfolk to pay taxes on everything they did. After many years, he declared himself the ruler and Baron of the surrounding lands.

"Arthus of Smythe had a son who grew up and some twenty years later, became a fine young man, much like his father. One day, when Iola was visiting one of the surrounding hamlets, the Baron's son was there too. She caught his eye. A short time later, he sought her out. At first, Iola showed no interest, but the more he pursued her, the more she fell for his charm and his kindness.

"His persistence paid off, and he too, became family. Mael gave his blessing and the two were married. He was a hard worker and fully committed himself to helping his new family. And, just like Iola, longevity started to flow through his veins too.

"All was well. Or so it seemed. You see, Cade, the son of Baron Arthus, now son-in-law to Mael, was not at all who he made himself out to be. He became very interested when he learned about the secrets of the White Tree, while he himself held secrets of his own. At first, it seemed nothing more than curiosity but then he wanted to know more. Every chance he got, he was around the White Tree, studying, learning, even trying to gain access by himself at times. Of course, he could never enter by himself, not without the Celtic Oval. All this inquisitiveness was a concern to Mael, but before he could confront him about it, Baron Arthus suddenly died.

"Iola's husband took the position of ruler and Baron then shut himself in the Keep, along with his wife. Months and months passed, no word came out from the Keep. No one entered, no one left. It was silent. Then one day a sound came out from within the Keep, like the blowing of a large horn. The gate of the Keep opened and the march of horses thundered out. They came with a purpose; they came for the White Tree.

"*Ewch i'r goeden!*" Mael alerted Cadarn and Seren. "It has begun".

They began to make their way to the White Tree. Cadarn picked up some tools to use as weapons, but Mael rebuked him. "No, Cadarn, no violence. Let's just get to the Tree."

"What's going on?" questioned Cadarn.

"It's your brother-in-law. He's after the Celtic Oval," he replied, "we must protect it at any cost."

Cadarn looked intensely at his father, "The Celtic Oval? What about Iola?"

"Don't worry, son, we'll find her," said Mael.

They ran through the woodlands towards the White Tree, as they heard the sound of horses closing in from the distance. Suddenly the way before them cleared itself, making it easier for them to get to the Tree. As they moved ahead, the path behind them filled itself in with thick foliage. "This is Iola's work," Mael called out, "come, together we can beat this."

Minutes later, Mael, Cadarn and Seren reached the White Tree. Ardwyadd was waiting for them, "I saw you all coming. Seren, here" he said, as he passed her the Celtic Oval, "let's get inside."

A blaze of fiery arrows shot through the air. Some simply bounced off the White Tree, others landed on the ground and the growing brush around them. Another wave of fiery arrows flew through the air. Then another. Soon the White Tree was engulfed in fire.

"What are we going to do?" cried Seren in fear, remembering the flames she had been trapped in, in the past.

Cadarn comforted her, "Hey now, my dear, we're safe in here. See, you cannot feel the heat of the flames. They will die down and burn themselves out. We will think of something that will get us out of this situation. Right Father?"

"Aye, that we will. That we will," Mael replied.

At that moment, a burst of power came out from within the Tree, its pulse rippled across the ground, extinguishing the flames that surrounded them. Birds of every kind were startled, they cawed and screeched, as they left their treetop perches. The horses rose up on their hind legs, neighing, knocking some of their riders to the ground. Still startled, the horses bolted off in different directions, some dragging their riders with them, who had their foot caught up in the stirrups. Those who were left picked themselves up, stunned and bruised.

"FOOLS! Get up" shouted a voice. "Get to the Tree." The Baron appeared behind them, on his black horse which snorted through its nose. "Let's go." He ordered as he trotted slowly past the riders, with his sword drawn. His countenance was dark, his face set like flint, focused and determined, with eyes resolute and piercing, fixed on one goal, to take over and take possession of the White Tree.

There they were, standing in the midst of the smoke rising from the embers surrounding the White Tree. They were armed with swords and axes. The Baron rode up on his horse, "MAEL!" he shouted, "Give it up. Give me the Celtic Oval. I'll take it by force if I have to."

Mael did not answer.

"You're a fool, Mael. Let me help you harness the full power of the White Tree. I know about this Rock, which the Tree stands upon. Aye, the Rock of the Celts. An ancient stone, full of mystery, it is. Used by sorcerers of old, it was. Now I am here to reclaim that which once was used by my ancestors. My father was weak, a non-believer, he forsook the power that flowed through his blood, denying the very authority of our name. But not I, my blood is thick. I hereby take back what my family forgot and lost."

The Baron raised his hand to signal his men. At once, with axes in hand, they swung at the White Tree. The axes however, bounced off without even making a mark, ringing with each swing. Again, they swung their axes. The sound of ringing filled the air, as each axe head ricocheted off the trunk of the Tree. Mael placed his hands on the inside of the Tree. They swung a third time. Thump, thump, thump, thump. As soon as the axe hit the trunk, the axe head dissolved into dust, leaving only the wooden handle in their hands. This infuriated the Baron.

"Mael," the Baron yelled, "You toy with me. You just do not understand the weight of what you are doing. Don't you forget, I have your daughter. Now give me the OVAL!"

Cadarn touched his father's shoulder and gasped. "Worry not, my son, he will not harm her." Mael whispered, "He needs her. We just need to come up with a plan."

Unknowingly to them, Ardwyadd had come up with a plan by himself. He had climbed up inside the Tree and open a portal by one of the high branches.

"Ardwyadd, no..." Mael called out. But it was too late.

Ardwyadd jumped down on top of the men below, catching them all by surprise, knocking one out. He grabbed two others and banged their heads together, knocking them out cold. Ducking and swiping he used his strength to knock out another. Suddenly he was jumped from behind, so Ardwyadd threw himself back on the White Tree, which was all he needed to free himself. Three more men attacked him all at once, but they were no match for his unusual feat of strength. He defeated them all.

The Baron clapped his hands, "Ardwyadd! The brave and strong."

At that moment, Ardwyadd lurched towards the Baron.

"But foolish" the Baron continued, as he stretched out

his hand and pulled it back as if going to throw something. However, a spear came from behind and plunged into Ardwyadd's back. Ardwyadd inhaled deeply, grabbing his chest. He stumbled a little, then recomposed himself, and lurched again towards the Baron.

Again, the Baron stretched out his arms and clapped his hands together, this time two spears flew into the air and plunged into Ardwyadd's right and left side. Tears screamed through Ardwyadds eyes in pain as he fell forward.

Mael, Cadarn, and Seren stood there in the Tree, tears streaming down their faces, crying in pain for their fallen son and brother.

"We've got to do something!" Cadarn said in grief. "We cannot let this carry on"

"Wait, son, wait," Mael replied, mournfully, trying to think of an answer.

Suddenly a light shone over where Ardwyadd lay. It was so bright it startled the Baron's horse, knocking him to the ground and ran off. Then the light faded and his body was gone.

Ardwyadd's Lifestone in the Celtic Oval glowed momentarily. "Don't give up, you will find a way." The voice of Ardwyadd echoed around them.

Grieved, Mael sorrowfully said, looking down. "Son, I have no choice now. There is a way, but it will take all that I have. You and your wife will have to time jump. I will send you into the future where all this will be forgotten and become folklore. And I will destroy the Celtic Oval." He said solemnly.

Cadarn looked painfully into his father's eyes, "It's…. it's…. it's all my fault…"

"NO, no son. Don't you ever think that. This is the fault of a man greedy for power. I should have seen this coming. I am the one who should have been more discerning. I am the one who failed." Mael corrected. "Now I have to fix this."

"MAEL!" shouted the Baron, "Come out! How many more lives need to be lost? Come mourn for your son."

Mael, still in grief said, "Cadarn, you are now the Keeper of the Tree. Wear your brother and sister's name, in honor of them." He opened up a door that led them nearly three hundred years into the future. "Go, my children. Go. This is one way only. I love you."

Seren hugged her father-in-law. Cadarn, with tears in his eyes and an ache in his heart, embraced his father for the last time. Mael kissed his cheek. "Son, you always were the daring one, that's what I loved about you most. Just like your mother." He smiled.

Mael gave the Celtic Oval to Seren, "Look after him, lasse." Cadarn and Seren stepped through the door, into the future. Once they were through Cadarn turned and gave the Celtic Oval to his father. Pain etched in both their eyes. "Good-bye, my son."

Mael's grief turned to anger, as he opened the portal to where the Baron stood.

"Well, well, well." The Baron gloated. "Look here."

"Silence your mouth." Mael snapped back. "You will pay for what you have done. You will never have what I possess. The White Tree will never yield its secrets to the likes of you. I will avenge the death of my son. If you so want the Celtic Oval, come and get it."

"You will die, along with your son, Mael. You are but an old man, weak and powerless." Sneered the Baron. He waved his hand and a sword flew into the air towards Mael. Mael held up his hand and the sword turned to dust in the air.

"You have to try harder than that." Mael taunted.

"Give me the Oval!" demanded the Baron

"NEVER!" Mael replied.

"Well maybe THIS will change your mind." said the Baron, as he motioned with his hand. Iola was brought before him. She was weak and limp, like she had been drugged.

"Leave her alone. I promise you this, if any harm comes to her, you will die." Mael said.

"Just give me the Celtic Oval and you will go free. You will both go free. I promise you." replied the Baron.

"I spit on your promises. Kill her and you will die. You are linked with her, with all of us, I'm sorry to say. But there will be a day when there will be retribution upon you, and all that you have done, will be undone. You have my word." Mael said with confidence. He reached into the White Tree and held the Celtic Oval in his hand. "You want this, but you will never have it. You will never have the honor of using it again."

Mael looked at his daughter, eyes weary and tired, his strength wavering. He turned and looked at Cadarn through the portals of the Tree one last time, and turned his head towards the Baron, as the Baron ran forward to take the Celtic Oval for himself. Mael closed his eyes and said, "O'r goeden daethoch chi, o'r goeden Rhaid i chi ddychwelyd." which means, 'From the Tree you came, to the Tree you must return'.

The Celtic Oval started to glow. Light shone out from around every Lifestone. One by one they came out and flew into the Tree.

"NO! NO! STOP THIS!" shouted the Baron. Still struggling with the Oval.

The Celtic Oval burned white hot, as they both screamed in pain. But not one of them let go. "You will never win," Mael said as he took the last stone from the Oval. "You are defeated."

The Baron fell to the ground clutching his right hand, as Mael rested against the White Tree and tossed what was left of the Oval into the Tree, where it disappeared.

Slowly the Baron picked himself up, blew into his hands and laughed mockingly, as his hand became like new, totally healed. "I underestimated you, Mael. I thought for sure you would give me the Celtic Oval. Now you have sealed your fate and the fate of your daughter. What a foolish man you are."

The Baron walked over to Mael and produced a dagger which he thrust into Mael's abdomen . "See, Mael. You die, I live. You lose, I win." and whispered in his ear, "I will return." And with that, Mael fell to the ground and the stone he had in his hand rolled onto the floor.

"NOOOOOOOOOOOOOO!" cried Cadarn, but there was nothing he could do. He fell back into his wife's arms and they both cried.

The ground on which the Baron stood, shook. A light swirled around Mael's body and a bright light suddenly shone all around and then it faded away and the body was gone.

The Baron picked up the stone, signaled his men and returned to Iola, back to the Keep. Neither one was ever seen again.

Over time, the Keep became a ruin as you see it today. Cadarn and Seren lived out their days in the future. They had a child of their own, who then grew up and married, had a child of their own and so on. Which brings us to where we are today."

Cade climbed on some of the stones that had fallen over time, looking this way and that, listening as he went. The entrance to the Keep looked as though something or someone had recently been there, as the tall grass that grew there had been trampled down. Cautiously, Cade entered the Keep. The high walls stood like giants as he ventured further into the darkness. Cade had brought an old oil lamp with him, he lit it and continued on. He made sure not to make any noise, as he had no idea what he was going to encounter. Then out of the silence, he heard a sound.

Quickly he ducked down and looked in the direction the sound came from. It was a voice, echoing down the halls of the Keep to his left. He took a gulp and headed slowly that way. As he drew close, the sound got louder and clearer. The voice was a man's voice, it sounded grave and deep. Cade blew out the light, not wanting to give his position away. As his eyes grew used to the dark, he saw a man pacing up and down, muttering and murmuring to himself. The man was over six foot tall, with thick black hair, he had a long thin face with a short beard. He was dressed in odd clothes, a black leather armored suit, with black pointed boots that came up to his knees. Around his waist was....a sword.

Cade tried to make out what this man was saying, but he used a dialect that he was not too familiar with. It was Celtic, old Celtic. A language he had not heard for many, many years. His grandpa used to teach him old Celtic when he was very young, but that was the last time he had heard it, until now, that is. However, the more he heard this man talk, the more he started to understand.

"What has become of this place?" the mysterious man said to himself, "I don't understand. Why would anyone leave it to ruin? Things have changed, yes, yes, but this. Hmph! This is unEXCEPTABLE!" He shouted.

This made Cade jump, knocking over the oil lamp and it rattled on the floor.

"Who's there, come on, speak," demanded the man, unsheathing his sword. "Show yourself!"

But Cade was too afraid and attempted to make a run for it. Suddenly the iron gates that hung on the walls closed, all by themselves. One by one, each gate closed, closing him in. Cade's heart was racing. Echoing in the stillness came footsteps, closer and closer they came until, out of the shadows, the man stood before Cade, sword drawn and pointed it towards him.

"AH, you are only but a wee boy!" he said tauntingly. "Let me see here." as he let the side of the blade of his sword slide down Cade's jacket.

Cade froze, unable to speak, just looking at the blade, trying to mouth the words.

"Ha ha ha! Cat got your tongue? Now, now. Hmmm, ah yes. I've seen your face before. Now let me think.... who is it now, Maelona, that's right. Maelona must be your mother...... and... Bryce, your father. Oh yes, such a valiant effort he made, but alas was outsmarted. Oh, don't worry he's fine......well.... sort of....at least for now." His every word pierced Cade. "So, young boy, son of Maelona, son of Bryce and grandson of.... Cadarn!"

'Cadarn?' thought Cade, 'no, it's Kai'. Anger started brewing inside of him. How he was going to get out of this, he did not know, but one thing he knew for sure, it was not going to end well.

"Oh, did I say something wrong?" the man replied to the look on Cade's face, "Be assured, my words are correc....." The man's sword suddenly flew out of his hand and rattled on the stone floor.

"MAXEN!" Shouted a voice from the darkness. "LEAVE THE BOY ALONE!"

"What! Who dares to interrupt ME!" the man, now named Maxen, replied back.

"Leave him alone" the voice in the dark demanded again.

"HA! You fool! You dare come oppose ME!" Maxen said smugly, pointing in the direction where the voice spoke. The sword flew into the air, this time heading straight towards the voice in the dark.

The voice in the dark clapped his hands together, catching the sword, turning it instantly into dust. "You're no match for me, Maxen! You do not belong here. Return what you've taken and release the boy."

"Only a coward hides in the shadows. Reveal yourself and I will let the boy go," Maxen said cunningly.

Maxen was met with silence.

"REVEAL YOURSELF, COWARD," Maxen shouted angrily as he stretched his hand out towards Cade, who was still on the floor. Cade clutched his chest. Pain gripped his body as he cried out, barely able to breathe, while the color started to drain from his face.

"Enough!" the voice in the dark spoke out. A strong gust of wind suddenly blew directly at Maxen, which knocked him off his feet, freeing Cade from this grip.

Cade gasped fresh air, as he stood up and started to run out of the place.

"Not so fast, boy!" Maxen demanded, brushing himself off as he stood back up.

Cade could not move. Something was holding his legs in place. Maxen laughed. "Ahhh, why such an interest in this boy's life. Makes one wonder..." He said as he walked around Cade. "Tell me, ...stranger, what value do you place on him? Do you really think that you have the upper hand? Ha, ha, ha. Surely not.

"I did not come here, ill-prepared. Only a fool would think that. But, oh voice in the shadows, you are very much mistaken. It is not this boy's life in the balance, but your own!"

Suddenly the walls of the Keep shook. Stones became

dislodged as they fell to the ground where they stood. The walls, where 'the voice in the shadows' stood, collapsed on top of him. Then there was silence.

Maxen laughed.

Cade looked towards the pile of rubble where the 'voice' had stood. He could not believe what he was seeing. It was a dream, a nightmare. Whatever it was, it was one he wanted to end.

"Now, BOY!" sneered Maxen, "what to do with the likes of you?"

A breeze swept across the floor and swirled around Cade's feet. Cade felt a release. The breeze grew into a mini cyclone that separated Cade from Maxen. The ground where Maxen stood started to give way, as he slowly sank into the ground.

The rubble over where the voice stood, crumbled into powder, as a figure appeared from out of the dust. "It's not over yet!" it said, as the voice walked into the light.

"Cadarn?!" exclaimed Maxen, wide-eyed.

"Grandpa!" Cade said in surprise, at the same time. "Wait, wha…"

"Cade, run. Get out of here. Go to the White Tree." His grandpa said.

"But…." Cade questioned.

"Yes Cade, I .... I am Cadarn. Can't explain now, just go. Go to the Tree. I'll be alright", said his grandpa.

Cade ran, as fast as he could, out of Byne Keep, leaving his grandpa, Kai, or rather Cadarn to deal with Maxen by himself.

"It's futile, you know." Laughed Maxen. "You lose; I win...again." as he released himself from the stone floor.

Cade ran, not knowing what direction he should take, but with each step he took, he moved closer. The skies above began to grow restless, as the clouds boiled over the hilltops, gathering in strength and blotting out the tranquility of blue that had calmed the day. Cade was met with silence, as nature around him seemed to hold its breath. A clap of thunder broke open the heavens, catching him by surprise, as he ducked down covering his head with his hands, still in full sprint. The wind picked up, as the sound of rain started to fall. Cade continued running. Another clap of thunder echoed all around, which seemed to urge the angry clouds to release all of their bounty at once. Thick, heavy drops of rain hit him across his face, wetting him almost instantly. Shielding his eyes, he continued forward. The ground beneath, sodden and flooding, could not keep up with the sudden downpour. It splashed up and muddied him, soaking his sneakers.

The rain was cold, heavy and unrelenting, as Cade made his way towards the canopy of trees up ahead. Here, once under the cover of the thick foliage above, the rain was detained from falling, as the leaves collected their fill, giving a small breather for Cade, below. He rested up against the trunk of a tree, catching his breath while wiping his forehead and slicking his rain-soaked hair back. He looked back towards Byne Keep, now in the far distance and shook his head as he breathed out slowly.

The rain danced on the leaves above, relentlessly trying to penetrate through the barrier. Cade straightened himself and carried on. Something inside of him was pulling him. Calling him. Drawing him. It was as if an inside compass was guiding him through the woodlands, moving him this way, then that. Up and over, he went, like water finding its way down a pane of glass. On and on he ran. The closer he got, the stronger the pull. The stronger the pull, the surer his steps were. As he drew near, his pace slowed. It was not long before he came to a small clearing and there it was, standing tall and strong, almost majestic looking. Its bark wet and glistening in the rain. Cade just stood there as the rain fell. He was here, he had arrived.

There it was, standing before him. Tall, regal and majestic. Its white brilliance shone brightly. Cade just stood there, in awe. So much history surrounded this Tree and now, he too, was caught up in it all. He had to find and rescue not only his dad but his mother too. How? He had no idea.

Chapter 7

❧ THE WHITE TREE ❧

The cold wind blew as the heavy rain continued to fall. Cade slowly walked around the White Tree stretching out his hands as if to touch it, but withheld from doing so, not knowing what was going to happen. His heart was beating fast, his breath was labored, a million thoughts ran rampant through his mind. Cade closed his eyes and let out a breath, which vaporized in the cold air around him, and turning his head slightly to the side, reached out his hand and touched the White Tree.

A brilliant bright light suddenly flashed from the Tree, as he touched it, knocking him back onto the ground. In that moment, Cade felt himself, as if in slow motion, fall back in what was like a sea of light. It sounded as if he was underwater, sinking but floating. Time seemed to stop and move, all in the same instance, as he hit the ground hard but softly. Cade opened his eyes with a start, gasping in deeply as he sat up as if he had just woken up from a bad dream, and looked around.

The air was warm. Gone were the heavy angry clouds above, gone was the relentless driving cold rain and the sound of the storm was silenced into stillness. The sun shone brightly, the air was fresh and fragrant. Nature's soft sound sang its chorus in a lulled and lazy fashion. In that short moment, Cade drank in the richness and freshness of it all, for it was nothing like he had ever experienced before. The White Tree stood before him, but something was different, something seemed out of place. Where were all the trees? They were gone. He was sitting in an open field next to a large rock that was embedded in the ground under the Tree. Cade rubbed his eyes, bewildered, then looked again.

"Fall into a river, did ya? Strange, there be no river near", a man's voice came from behind.

Cade shot up like an arrow, confused and a little dazed, almost knocking himself off balance, as he spun around.

"Steady there, now", the man said, as he reached out his hand to steady him.

"Whoa, wha...no I'm ok, I'm...er..." Cade stammered, still in shock.

The man smiled. "Aye, well...", he was interrupted by the cries of a baby behind him on a small cart that was pulled along by a donkey. "Excuse me," he said, as he turned to tend to the baby. The man picked up his child, and said, "There, there, boy. No cause for yer fussin' now. Papa's here, Papa's here."

He turned around to Cade, "I'd like you to meet my lil' boy 'ere, named him Cadarn, oh and these two", he said pointing into the cart, "are Ardwyadd and my lil' girl, Iola. My name's Mael."

Cade, stood there, frozen, still dripping from the rain, his eyes wide, with a puzzled and confused look on his face, mouthing inaudible words.

"It's ok, take yer time. Come, sit down, before you fall down. Listen, I knows who you are and why you were sent here. I been waiting for you." Mael said.

Cade sat down slowly, absorbing everything, his mind abuzz, still a little bewildered, he looked around and took a deep breath. The air was clear, crisp and clean. He took another deep breath in through his nose and slowly exhaled out his mouth. The fresh smell of green was intoxicating, it enlivened every neuron in his body. It helped him clear his mind a little, as he arranged the thoughts in his mind in order, like files in a computer.

His thoughts wandered to his father and his quest, then on to his mother's disappearance, and finally his grandfather's words, which swirled around inside of him. Next flashed the struggle within Byne Keep between his grandpa and the Baron, where he had just come from. "Grandpa!" he called out.

"Aye, steady yerself lad", Mael reassured him, but that sudden outburst startled baby Cadarn and he started crying again. "Ere, lad, take the baby, maybe you can settle yourselves, eh"

Cade took the baby in his arms, nervously but gently, and smiled a little. "So you're my grandpa, huh!", "how can this all be?" he whispered into the baby's ear. It did seem very unbelievable.

Mael laughed. "Many a secret this Tree has, boy. Many it has. Learned a lot I 'ave too, in all these 'ere years. Now the Tree has brought us together, through what?" raising his eyebrows, "hundreds of years, 'undreds of 'em. Why? Hmm, to right a wrong, that 'appened in my future, and in your past. You're here to learn the ways of the White Tree, to unlock secrets that I could never open. 'Tis my duty to protect the family. To teach and instruct them to live and succeed in this 'ere life. To be 'umble an' all and never wielding our gift as a means of gain or power.

"I don't know all the reasons or the 'appenings that led you 'ere, never-the-less, we're here in the now, and now we prepare."

Mael stood up and turned to tend to the other two babies, "Oh, and one more thing, don't you worry about Cadarn. That there baby, your grandpa, as it were, will be just fine. Believe me, whatever he's facing, he's strong enough and clever enough to take care of himself. Come along, now, there's work to be done. An' anyhow, we got to get you dry and out of those funny fancy clothes of yours and into summin' more proper, eh?"

Cade looked down at what he was wearing, it did seem out of place for when he was. He grinned to himself as he shook his head a little, "Come on grandpa," he said in baby Cadarn's ear, as he followed behind Mael, leading the way.

He could not believe how different everything looked. There were rolling grasslands as far as the eye could see, with only a few small trees here and there. Over in the distance, he could clearly see Byne Keep, only now, it was not a ruin at all, like he had known. It stood tall and strong, overlooking the hills and the meadows, like a watchman standing over its territory.

Mael, with two babies tucked safely into the crook of his arm and hand, laid his free palm on the trunk of the White Tree and uttered some words Cade did not quite hear, and a door appeared and opened before him. "Come on lad", Mael motioned his head inside as he stepped into the Tree, disappearing from sight.

Cade stood there, holding baby Cadarn, just looking at the Tree. He looked down again at the baby, thinking that he was in some sci-fy movie, as it all seemed so surreal. However, he took a breath and said to himself, "you got this", and stepped into the White Tree himself.

Once inside, Cade was amazed by what he saw. It was not anything at all like he imagined it to be, not that he had really imagined what it would be like. He never envisaged it having much space, but it did; lots of space. The walls of the tree trunk appeared to be semi-transparent from the inside, which slowly pulsated in a kind of electric white glow. Dancing sporadically within the walls were what seemed like veins of lightning, running up and down every other second or so. It was very bright inside but it did not hurt your eyes or make you squint, but rather, it woke up your eyes as you drank it all in.

"Ere laddie", Mael said, pointing to a small crib-like cradle and breaking Cade's new awareness, "Rest Cadarn down 'ere.". Ardwyadd and Iola lay sleeping in the two other cradles next to the empty. As soon as Cade laid baby Cadarn down, he cooed and giggled a little before nodding off to sleep.

"Ha! Works every time, it does." chuckled Mael, "every time. Just like that," as he snapped his fingers. "Anyhows, before we do anything else, you need to be changing outta those wet clothes of yours. Down there, first door on yer right. There be something for you to dry yerself and change an' all. Meet me 'ere when you done change."

Cade walked down and entered the first room on the right. He pulled on the sackcloth curtain that hung across the doorway, draping it across the door and looked around the small room. Here, the walls were more opaque, though they still pulsated in the same manner as they did in the main area, with the veins of lightning flowing up and down. It was quite mesmerizing to see. Cade took a closer look and reached out his hand a few centimeters from the wall, not touching it, but then retracted his hand back quickly, remembering what happened the first time he touched the White Tree.

A few minutes later Cade returned to the main area where Mael was waiting for him.

"Ahh! There you are." Mael said, "you looks like you fit

in now 'cept you all a little too clean around the edges eh, for our kinda livin'. None to worry. Won't be long, I'm sure."

Cade was dressed in a pair of light brown trousers that tied with a cord around the waist, a tan and gray v-necked long sleeved shirt and a dark brown long-tailed vest that came down to just above his knee. On his feet, he wore a pair of soft black boots that came up to his shins.

"I know I's been done all the talkin' and all, an' this 'ere is new to you, but you 'ave no need to worry yerself." Mael reassured him, "You with family 'ere, and er, call me a mule, but I's never got yer name, laddie, with the babies fussin' an all, when we met."

"Oh, it's...it's Cade. I'm Cade" replied Cade extending his hand.

Mael reached out and took hold of Cade's wrist, pulled him close and patted him on the back. "Welcome Cade, welcome," Mael said. "Now Cade, first things first, it's time for you to get acquainted with the Tree. Put yer 'and on 'ere," he said, pointing to a cylinder pedestal that stood in the center of the White Tree, "then close yer eyes."

Cade hesitated.

"It be alright, laddie." encouraged Mael, "go on."

Cade took a deep breath, stretched out his hand, closed

his eyes and placed his palm on the pedestal.

Immediately a burst of light pulsed out from under his hand and Cade opened his eyes. The room he was standing in was much larger, so large that it looked like it had no end, and now he stood alone. His skin was somewhat illuminated and the same energy flow that he saw in the walls of the White Tree was now flowing through him. Cade looked at his hands front to back slowly, as they tingled ever so slightly like when he had pins and needles from hitting his funny bone, except there was no numbness.

"What the..." Cade whispered.

Then gravity gave up its grip and Cade left the ground beneath him and floated in mid-air. Above him formed something like a whirlwind, a force of spinning light and energy, which descended upon him, then surrounded him. He saw pictures and scenes appear before him, in a time-lapse fashion, of what was, and of what was to come. He saw the rise and fall of people in power, kings and kingdoms, past and present, then it faded. Next, he saw scenes of his childhood. He saw his Father, his grandparents, he saw a young woman...his mother? Then like an old 8mm videotape reel, the scene ended and there he was again, standing with his hand on the pedestal with Mael still standing next to him.

"Now Cade," Mael said, "now your training begins."

Chapter 8

❧ GIFTED ❧

If time-lag was such a thing, Cade had it. His whole world and timeline had been re-adjusted. Everything was different. Everything had changed. He almost felt like he was the third person looking into a scene from a book or a movie, but this was real, and he was here. His real being was in real-time, and the past he had read in the history books was his now, this was reality. How long? He did not really know but he accepted the fact that he was here.

The experience he had in the White Tree helped too, it connected him ever more deeply to his family and his family's past, giving him a greater understanding of who he was. The teachings he was getting from Mael, his great-grandfather, reminded him of J.R.R. Tolkien and the stories he had written.

Cade's mind was more alive than it had ever been before. Sure, these teachings were ancient old school, but his technological mind just connected all the dots and brought a perspective he had never seen before. The speed at which he was learning amazed Mael, as he grasped a hold of everything. Cade himself, was surprised to be able to fully understand and read the old Celtic language, as he vaguely remembered learning it for a short time when he was very young. His grandfather used to show him some ancient old books, long since tattered, similar to these, only these books were not so old and they were well kept.

Mael had books filled with old writings, most of which, if not all, had been written by him. Each page was filled with findings, etchings and formulas that worked and even those that did not work. It was important to know both. Such were the ways of the alchemist, which, of course, Mael was. He found ways to harness the power of and even manipulate not just metals, but wood and stone too. Through his time spent in the White Tree, Mael was able to learn more skills and influence the elements: - earth, wind, fire and water. Not that Mael had mastered every area, as it took much concentration and stamina but he was at least able to control them in part.

"Cade, learning is one thing, practice is another!" Mael said. "It's in the doin', does one practice. And in doin', you discover where your greater gift lies. Once you know what that is, you water it, you feed it and you watch it grow. It becomes a strength in you, and that strength, its purpose, is to serve and protect those around you. Never for self-gain, never for self-wealth, never for self-power. For if you do it for those there reasons, it will become your undoing, and it will own you. Eventually, you will lose all that you know, even your own self. This ain't no small matter, young Cade, so take heed. Learn, grow and master your strengths. Serve and protect, freely and without reward. This is our way.

"There are many here, up and down these lands that call what I do, magic. But a sorcerer, I am not... *we* are not. Rest assured, there be those who do practice magic, conjuring up twisted and dark ways of alchemy, surrendering themselves to evil an' all." Mael paused for a while, "Well, I'm guessin' when you're from, all this sound like tales and fables, eh? But it be true. You just being 'ere proves that! Now, let's put into practice that stuff you been reading about, eh? Come on, let's go."

Mael lead Cade into another room inside the White

Tree. There were seven white pedestals that stood in a semi-circle, each one bearing a different symbol, depending on its element. The first pedestal represented Wood, the second, Metal, the third, Stone, the fourth, Earth, the fifth, Wind, the sixth, Water and the seventh was Fire.

"Here, we find out which of these elements will become your strength. Of course, you will be able to learn to harness all of them but in varying degrees. It will take a lifetime to master each and every one of them, if indeed that is at all possible, which I, in my long life have not yet been able to accomplish." said Mael. He called out the names of each element. As he did so, they appeared, like the lighting of a candle, and they hovered above in their respected places. "So, which one will you choose first?" asked Mael.

Cade stood there and looked around at all the elements hovering above their own pedestal, and made his decision. He walked over to the second one and picked up the element. At once, the other six elements vanished, like someone had blown out the candles, and the pedestals descended and disappeared back into the floor. Cade spun around to Mael and held up his choice.

"Metal! Very interesting." remarked Mael, "Good choice. Now, what are you going to do with it?"

Cade looked at the metal cube in his hand and hoped this was where Mael stepped in, but instead, he had to remember what he had read in the alchemy books. In his mind, Cade turned the pages of the books he studied and then it came to him.

He held out the metal cube between his thumb and index finger and concentrated. At first, nothing happened. Then slowly the metal cube started to soften its edges as if to turn into a sphere, but then it suddenly got too hot for him to hold. "Ow!" he yelled out, dropping the cube on the floor. Cade looked at Mael while shaking his hand and blowing his fingers cool.

Mael laughed. "First lesson, metal gets hot when changing its composition."

Cade gave him a 'now-you-tell-me' stare and smirked.

"You thinking of this as a solid, which 'course it is. No, you need to think of it as a liquid, not like molten metal, mind you," Mael said, "lest you want to burn your 'ands off. More like liquid metal, you know, summin' that's soft and pliable, like clay."

Cade bent down and picked up the metal cube again. "Like a liquid," he whispered to himself. He placed the cube into the center of his hand and again began to concentrate on it. "Like a liquid" he silently mouthed the words.

The cube just sat there, in his hand. It felt cool. Cade closed his eyes and slowly opened them again. Then, just like an ice cube sitting in the hot sun, the metal cube started to melt. Slowly at first, then it sped up. Soon Cade had a pool of liquid metal in his cupped hand. He then tipped the liquid metal from one hand to the other and as he did, it formed a solid metal ball. Cade looked up with a big grin on his face.

Mael laughed. "Now that, my boy, was impressive!" patting Cade on the shoulder, "There's much more to learn, young one, much more. But this, this is a great start." Mael took the round metal ball from Cade's hand and placed it back on the pedestal, changing it back to its original form. The other six pedestals rose up from the floor and their elements appeared above them. "Now, young Cade, choose another."

"But I..." Cade began to say.

Mael held up his hand, "Time, we have none. Learn, you will. What you just did, took me years, it did, years I tell ya. You did it in a mere moment (snapping his fingers). There's more to you than you know. Come on, choose another."

Wood was his second choice, and just like they did before the other pedestals dissolved into the floor.

"Alright, Cade. Show me what you can do." Mael asked.

Like before, Cade flipped through the pages in his mind and found what he wanted to do. He focused his mind. This time he kept his eyes open as he held the piece of wood in his fist. Suddenly it began to grow. You could hear the splintering of wood as it stretched out into a staff, almost as tall as Cade. It was beautiful and ornate with carvings and etchings on it near the top end and towards the bottom it tapered into a rounded point.

"You got some imagination!" Marveled Mael, "Absolutely amazin'."

Cade rested the staff on the pedestal and, like before, the other six appeared in its place.

"Go on," said Mael. "Pick another"

Cade did.

With each choice, he was able to manipulate the element. With water, he turned it into ice; stone changed into sand and with wind, he was able to create a mini tornado in the palm of his hand. Earth and fire were next, but Cade was getting tired.

"I think you done enough for today, Cade." Said Mael, "You have done more than I could ever have thought you could have done. The next two elements are much harder to harness. Great destruction they can cause if mishandled. You are tired, and you must rest. We shall remain here for the night. Tomorrow is a new day. Tomorrow we shall continue. Your journey has just begun, and the steps you have taken today have only taken you a little way. I must say, I am impressed, you have done more than well, but don't let it go to your head. There's folly in pride and impatience, for they only lead to ruin. But, I see in you great things, young Cade, great things. You certainly are gifted. We shall do this one step at a time. Good night lad, till the morrow."

Chapter 9

❧ THE NIGHT IN THE TREE ❧

It was not the most comfortable, but it was better than sleeping on the floor. Cade was back in the room where Mael told him to dry off and change into something more time appropriate. The bed was made of moss, straw and strips of cloth, which tied it all together, making a kind of simple mattress. Two folded blankets sat at the foot of the bed.

Cade wrapped his modern day clothes, which he had draped over a chair to dry, around his backpack and rested it under his head for a pillow. As soon as he laid down, the room darkened and left only a faint glow around the edges of the walls, floor and around the doorway. Cade lifted his head slightly, amazed again at what had just happened, and smiled to himself as he laid back down. All was silent. Cade closed his eyes and fell asleep.

The cries of a baby woke him. He lazily sat up, rubbed his eyes and went to see if everything was ok. The 'lights' stayed dim as he made his way back into the main area, where Mael and the triplets were sleeping, well, all but one of them. Cade bent down and cradled the one that was crying, it was Cadarn.

"Hey there, grandpa" whispered Cade, "It's ok, shhhh, I'm here now", holding him close to his chest, lulling him back to sleep. The others did not stir. "There, there, there's a good boy, Cade's here, shhh, shh..." Cadarn quieted down and started softly cooing. Just then, Cade noticed a light appear down the hall. Intrigued, he walked over to it find it was the training room. 'Odd', he thought, "Shall we go in?" he whispered to baby Cadarn, to which he gave a small giggle. "Ok then, grandpa, let's go," Cade replied. Once inside, the room lit up from one end to the other, as if the lights were being switched on, row by row, but of course, the White Tree had no lights, or light switches, for that matter. The doorway, which he walked through, closed up and the seven pedestals arose from the floor in a semi-circle, just as they did before. "What's going on?" he whispered again into baby Cadarn's ear; the baby just looked at him with a cheeky smile. "Yeah, yeah" Cade replied, "I know, you're only a baby."

Cade ventured further into the room. A small crib-like cradle formed next to him from out of the floor and a light shone from it. Cade whispered to baby Cadarn, "I guess I have to lay you down now." Baby Cadarn just smiled back. Cade gently laid Cadarn into the crib and said, "Don't you go anywhere, lil' guy" with a smile. "OK", as Cade went to turn away, Baby Cadarn grabbed a hold of Cade's little finger. In that instant, it was as if time suddenly stopped then rushed forward like a flood and he was standing in front of his grandpa, just like he'd known him from the future, old and grey, wise and kind.

"Cade!" Welcomed his grandpa, Kai. "Good to see you. Come, wipe that look off your face, it's me, it's your ol' grandpa."

Cade was speechless.

Grandpa Kai, chuckled, "'S ok, young Cade. Many things may seem confusing from time to time but worry not. You'll get your 'ed around it, you will. You got a strong 'eart and a clever 'ed. Just don't think too hard eh? Anyways, I forgot to give you this," as he handed Cade a small beaded necklace. "It's your mother's." With that, time rushed back to where he was, and baby Cadarn let go of Cade's finger.

Chapter 10

• FIRE! •

Cade woke refreshed and ready for his day. He was surprised he did not feel achy. He remembered the campouts he used to have with his dad when he was young, and how the sleeping bag did not give enough comfort from the ground below. Not that he minded then, it was fun and adventurous.

He stood up on his knees to make the bed when a small blue beaded necklace fell onto the floor. Cade picked it up slowly, "It was not a dream," he said to himself, a little taken aback.

The necklace was made up of a thin leathery weaved band with small beads varying in size, with varying shades of blue going through it. He wrapped it around his wrist and was able to tie it together with one hand, and tucked it under his shirtsleeve. If it belonged to his mother, then he wanted to keep it safe.

"*Bore Da!* Decided to wake, eh?" Mael teased. "Well, 'ave yerself a bite or two of this 'ere laverbread and," pointing to a bucket of water, "splash yer face so we can continue yer trainin' an all."

"Good morning," replied Cade, "thank you."

He took a bite of the laverbread, it was not quite the same as the way his grandma made it, this was coarser and a little chewy, but still tasted good. He looked up at Mael. Here was his great-grandfather who, according to the story his grandpa told him, was over ninety years old by the time he had these children. Of course, he did not look much older than thirty years old. Mael was lean and strong, about 5' 10" and had black/brown hair. He wore a beard well. His smile was soft, which reminded him of his grandpa. When he spoke, his words seemed to stir in him a strength that he did not know he had.

"Well, young Cade. Sleep well?" Mael asked

"Yeah," he said clearing his throat, "yes I did, thanks. Something happened last night, I..."

Mael interrupted, "One thing, I must say laddie, without being rude or soundin' impertinent, but anything you see and hear is for you. I need not know. Can't help you beyond what I's know anyways, and I need not know about things that 'appen from the future. My assignment is already set, yours is still being mapped out. Come, finish up, we got work to do."

Cade ate the last of his laverbread, washed his face, looked at the triplets and said, "Bore da, Ardwyadd, bore da, Iola," then bent closer to baby Cadarn and whispered, "how'd that happen last night?", but baby Cadarn just answered with a giggle and a smile. "Hmm, guess you're not gonna tell, huh?" He said with a grin, "See you all later."

Mael stepped back into the main room, "E-ar', take these," as he handed Cade a sack full of what felt like dirt and twigs. "Gotta get these into the ground, come on," he continued, as he grabbed another sack.

Once outside, Cade breathed in the morning air. It made him feel so alive. It smelled fresh, sweet and clean. He could not get over how everything looked so very different.

"Come now, Cade, help me out 'ere," said Mael. "Got plantin' to do, and four 'ands are better than two!"

Mael had already broken up some of the land around the White Tree and planted a few tree saplings. Then it struck him, this was what his grandpa told him about. Mael was planting trees, which created the forest he knew, in order to hide the White Tree. Cade felt honored to be a part of history, even if it was in a small way.

Hours had passed and they had progressed quite a lot.

"Ok, Cade, next lesson. Help us along a bit." Mael said, "Earth is your next element and there's a whole lot of it here. Just focus on a small section and see what you can do, eh?"

Cade switched gears, in his mind he pulled out the books that he had studied and flipped through the pages once again. He looked up at Mael then looked back down at the ground, placing his right hand in the soil, and concentrated. The ground around his hand started to shake.

"Steady there laddie," Mael cautioned, "Focus on the small area around you, don't wanna shake up the whole place now."

Cade nodded, and sure enough, only the small patch of land where he was continued to shake. Then slowly the ground began to churn up slightly, as he focused more directly, like someone was tilling it. Then he stopped.

"Excellent! See, you did it." Mael encouraged.

Cade wiped the sweat from his forehead, "I... I guess I

did." He replied.

"Only one more to go, but first I got to take care of the babies. I'll leave you 'ere to finish this section off, won't be far if you needs me." Mael said, "When I get back we'll tackle the final element."

Cade took a break and drank some water from the bucket Mael had brought out for him. It was cold and refreshing, pure and crisp. He looked out on the rolling countryside, trying to fathom the extent of the work that had to be done. There sure were miles and miles of tree planting to do, and it would take years, but then Cade remembered, Mael had plenty of time, *did* have plenty of time. He smiled to himself and went back to planting the tree saplings.

When the last sack was empty, Cade sat back and stretched his arms, he had put in a full day's work and was tired.

"Now you fit in." came a voice behind him, it was Mael. "Did a real good job there, Cade, really good job," patting him on the shoulder. "Here you go, I fixed you summin' to eat," handing him a plate full of potatoes, laverbread and vegetables.

Cade thanked him and started eating.

Mael stared into the distance, "Your time here is nearly

up, Cade. It's been real good meeting you." His voice was quiet. "Fact is, you bein' 'ere's 'elped me. You know, losing the one you love physically is a terrible loss. But knowin' too she's here, in our children, and in part, in you, brings comfort.

"You know, this 'ere tree was birthed from her tear! Marvelous thing it was. We never knew how or why, it just was. Healed her it did. And many years it gave us together too, many years…. Anyways, young Cade, finish up." he said, clearing his throat, "one more lesson, one more element to go."

Cade felt privileged to be here and to hear the voice of Mael for himself. He proposed to do his best to save, restore and bring honor to his family's legacy. "I'm ready." Cade said.

The sun was starting to set and the darkness of the night began to creep over the rolling countryside. Mael struck two flint stones together and lit some kindling on the end of a torch. "There," he said, "the hardest and the greatest element of all. It requires utmost concentration. Don't fear it, don't think lightly of it. Respect it." He passed the flaming torch to Cade.

Cade stood there, his eyes reflecting the flickering of the flame, licked his lips, while once again flipping through the pages of the books in his mind. His breathing was labored, his palms started to sweat a little. He gulped, then stretched out his hand holding the torch and focused on the flame. For a moment it flickered like normal, but then it suddenly burst forth, like a flamethrower that spits liquid into the flame to make it shoot out and intensify. This startled Cade; he stepped back and let go of the torch. It landed on one of the sacks, which immediately burst into flames, igniting the other sacks lying next to it. This then frightened the donkey, which started braying loudly and tried to bolt, but could not as he was tied to a post in the ground.

Cade was panicked and attempted to contain the fire, but could not calm his mind down. He stretched out his hand to calm the flames but actually made it worse; the flames shot out like a flamethrower and burnt some of the tree saplings he had planted that day. The fire was getting out of hand. However, Mael clapped his hands together, then opened his arms wide and rain appeared out of nowhere, extinguishing the fire, leaving only smoldering embers r. Then Mael went over to the donkey and calmed it down.

"Sorry, sorry, I just coul...." Cade began to say.

"'S-ok. No harm done...apart from those saplings

there." Mael interrupted, "Told you fire was a lot more difficult." He smiled. "None to worry."

"But..." Cade said

"None to worry!" Mael insisted, interrupting again. "Another day, eh."

"Ok, yeah, another day," Cade replied.

Mael smiled, "Remember, everything your doing is for the greater good. Well, need to be tending to the younglings. Till the morrow." He said, as he entered the White Tree.

Cade picked himself off the floor and dusted himself off, looking around at the faint glow of the embers on the ground, pursed his lips and shook his head. "Tomorrow's another day." He said to himself and walked up to the White Tree to enter it. However, when he touched it, a bright light burst forth, knocking him to the floor, and just like before, he felt himself in a sea of light, falling but not falling. Time seemed to stop and move all in the same instance, as he hit the ground hard but softly. He opened his eyes, it was still night.

"Hey you!" a voice whispered loudly, "come with me."

A large heavy set man with broad shoulders stood

above him, "The name's Ardwyadd" he said, as he ran off into the thick woods.

FIRE!

Chapter 11

❧ ARDWYADD ❧

Cade found himself in the woods again. The light from the moon above was just enough to see the grey tree shadows around him. Before he could think another thought, Cade, for some unknown reason, got up and followed the man who called himself Ardwyadd. It did not take very long, however, before he realized that he seemed now to be alone in the woods. Cade stopped and listened for a moment. He heard nothing. Where did Ardwyadd go? If indeed, it was Ardwyadd. It did not take a genius to figure out that he had jumped time again, for he felt the same way he had felt before. The rush of everything caught up with him when suddenly a man jumped down from above, causing Cade to yell out and fall back. The man before him laughed.

"Here, take my hand", the man said.

Hesitantly Cade extended his arm and allowed the man to help him up.

"Ardwyadd?" questioned Cade.

"That's me! And you, you are...?" said Ardwyadd.

"Cade!" They said together.

"Huh?" Cade said, kind of surprised.

"I knew you were coming. I saw it a few days ago when I was alone in the White Tree. It showed me." said Ardwyadd. "Here, I have something for you."

Ardwyadd stood almost six-foot-tall, with thick arms and legs to match. He was dressed in animal firs and looked every bit of a rough and rugged rugby player, with unkempt long brown hair, but he had a kind face and a reassuring smile. Reaching behind him, he grabbed a long pole-like object wrapped in cloth, which he had strapped to his back.

"Here," said Ardwyadd, "this belongs to you", handing it over to Cade.

A little mystified, Cade took the package. He bent down on his knees and unfolded the cloth to reveal what it was. Cade's eyes grew large. It looked aged, but there lying on the ground was the staff that he had created from that small piece of wood on the pedestal in the White Tree. He remembered when Mael had told him to 'see what he could do' when learning about the elements and how to manipulate them.

"Every one of us has a gift, an ability. One that is especially greater and stronger than the rest. Your second choice was wood. You connected with it, and with it, you created what you see before you." informed Ardwyadd. "That staff is as much a part of you, as you are of it. Take hold of it and don't let it leave your side."

Cade picked up the staff. As he did, it was as if a new lease of life was breathed into it.

"There now," said Ardwyadd, "it's time to learn to defend yourself."

"Defend myself?" quizzed Cade.

"Yes!" Ardwyadd replied, as he suddenly attacked Cade with a pole that he carried behind his back.

Cade blocked the blow with his staff.

"Good reflexes," said Ardwyadd, a little surprised, and attacked again.

Cade blocked it again.

"What are you doing?" Cade said as he fended off the attacks.

"For you to make it out here, you have to learn to

defend yourself," answered Ardwyadd, as he continued to attack. This time Ardwyadd got a hit in, knocking Cade to the ground.

Ardwyadd extended his hand to help him up. "Thanks", said Cade.

As soon as Cade got up, Ardwyadd attacked again, knocking Cade back to the floor. Like before, Ardwyadd extended his hand and laughed, "Come on, you're not even trying." said Ardwyadd.

Cade just looked at him and held out his hand. "It's not exactly fair, you're what, three times bigger and stronger than me?" He retorted.

Ardwyadd smiled as he let out a breath through his nose. "That may be, but life can be bigger than both of us. What you going to do? Sit back and let it smack you around? No, if you are to fear that which is before you, you will always be beaten by it. See beyond what is in front of you. Every mountain can be climbed once you assess it and find a foothold. Challenging? Yes! Impossible? No!

"Sometimes you got to think quick, but the same always applies, assess and find a foothold, climb the mountain, conquer the giant. Second important thing is to hold on. Yes, you may slip and fall sometimes and feel the bumps and bruises that come as a result of it, but hold on. Take a breath, refocus, learn where you went wrong and carry on. That's the third important lesson, keep going. Sometimes it doesn't work out the way you thought, sometimes it may feel like it is all too much, but don't stop. Don't let it defeat you, keep on going. You can do it. Now, keep going!" as Ardwyadd went into attack mode again.

Cade and Ardwyadd continued to spar it out. With each blow, Cade got more and more confident as staff and rod knocked together. Back and forth they went, sometimes ducking out the way, sometimes jumping over a swing. "There you go!" said Ardwyadd, "That's the way." As they continued, Cade began to notice that even though Ardwyadd was heavy set, he was not so agile on his feet. Then when the time was right, he took the opportunity. He ducked left and right, then did a forward roll and with a quick swipe of his staff, knocked Ardwyadd off his feet. As Cade rolled sideways out of the way, he knocked the rod out of Ardwyadd's hands. He quickly stood up and thrust the staff close to Ardwyadd's head as he let out a victory cry.

A little out of breath, Ardwyadd smiled, "Well, well. Guess I'm beaten."

"Guess so!" panted Cade.

"Here, help me up." said Ardwyadd.

As Cade went to help him up, Ardwyadd grabbed Cade's arm and pulled him close, raised his foot up and toss kicked Cade over himself. "Ha, ha, find a foothold," chuckled Ardwyadd as he picked himself up, "or in this case, a foot toss."

"Not fair," said Cade, "I won!"

"Winning isn't the aim of the game," Ardwyadd replied.

Cade saw that he had dropped his staff, which was now lying on the floor next to Ardwyadd's feet. He closed his eyes and flipped through the pages of the books Mael had given him to study, then, as in slow motion, he opened them again and stretched out his hand. The staff moved, then spun, like a helicopter blade. It completely took Ardwyadd by surprise and knocked him off his feet again. Ardwyadd, with his feet and arms flailing, fell to the ground with a thump. The ground shook, as the leaves plumed around his fallen body then floated softly back to the ground. Cade's staff returned to his hand as he stood with a big grin on his face.

"You were right! It's not about winning." Cade said teasingly.

"Good call. Good call." Ardwyadd said nodding his head in surrender.

The sun was beginning to rise. "Well time to head back

to the White Tree," said Ardwyadd. "I got things to do."

"But, we've only just started," Cade said

"Aye, well. You got what you needed." replied Ardwyadd

"But I got questions," said Cade.

"That may be." Responded Ardwyadd, "but I can't answer any of 'em. You're a smart lad. Skilled you are. You're more than you know. Don't you worry. Trust me, all your questions will get their answers soon enough. Just remember all that you learned here, and you'll do well."

Cade conceded. "You're right. Oh, and thank you." He said

"Hey, been my pleasure, it has." Ardwyadd replied, "just another step towards accomplishing your destiny. Everything we do is for the greater good. Oh, and remember, that there staff is to stay by your side."

Cade looked at the staff on his right, then looked back at Ardwyadd, but he had disappeared. Cade looked high and low. 'How could a guy that big just disappear like that?', Cade thought to himself. After a short while looking around, he realized that he was alone again, Ardwyadd was gone, nowhere to be found.

The sun was beginning to rise as wind in the trees above started to blow harder which made the leaves rustle.

Just then, he heard a snapping sound a little way from where he was standing. Someone or something was coming his way.

Chapter 12

❧ THE WOODEN HUT ❦

The morning skies brought a shift in the atmosphere as dark clouds bubbled up over the hillside. Thunder began to roll gently across the canopy of trees above. The wind picked up as the branches swayed back and forth, causing the leaves to rustle. The air changed and the smell of wet blew through the trees. A shiver went up Cade's spine as he knelt there, looking and searching with his eyes, fully expecting Ardwyadd to surprise him again. Then out from the shadows of the trees came a tall figure wearing what looked like a long shawl or cape, which had a hood that covered the face of whoever was approaching him.

Cade's heart beat a little faster as he gulped, fixing his

eyes on the person walking towards him.

"I remember you," said a soft voice. "I know your face. Don't be alarmed, come...come from your hiding."

Cade did not move.

"I understand that you are wary, but you have nothing to fear. You have been taught much, and much you have achieved in such a small period of time. And while it may seem like you have time in abundance, you do not, hence the urgency of your training." The mystery figure walked slowly up to where Cade was. "Don't you remember me? Don't you remember greeting me with a 'bore da', early in that day, so many years ago?"

Cade slowly got to his feet and peered at the figure. Then his eyes widened, "Iola?" he guessed.

"Yes, yes! You are right." as she unveiled her head from the hood. "Do you know how long I've been waiting to return your salutation, ha ha, too long." She smiled. "Bore da, Cade, bore da!"

"Good morning to you too, I...Iola," said Cade.

Iola was almost the same height as Cade. She had brown eyes and long brown hair and wore a long brown hooded robe that came down to her ankles. She seemed a little mysterious, but her voice was gentle and calm.

"Come with me, Cade. The rains are about to fall. You

have one more step before your true adventure begins." said Iola. "and I for one, don't want to be standing in the rain."

It was not long before Cade and Iola reached their destination. They stood before an old fallen tree that had broken in several places. An ivy bush had taken over the area; it had almost completely covered it, like a spider's web marking its territory. Iola waved her hand and the finger stems of the ivy bush formed an archway, revealing a small wooden door.

"Come," she said.

Cade followed her as he ducked down under the archway, closed the door behind him and looked around.

"Welcome." Iola said, "It's a bit small, but it'll keep us dry from the rain."

Cade scanned the room with his eyes, it reminded him of his tree fort, only this was constructed from old strips of bark and crudely cut logs, which were held together with mud and moss. One of the walls of the wooden hut was the fallen tree that he had seen outside. Carved into that trunk were cubbyholes, which held all sorts of bottles and jars varying in size and color, all filled with different liquids and materials.

There was a table and a chair, both made from various

pieces of wood and branches. Growing up and around the roof of the wooden hut was an ivy plant, such as he had never seen before. In fact, it was quite amazing, for somehow this ivy produced a yellow/green glow. There was so much of it that it was enough to light up the whole place. Cade reached up and touched one of the leaves, instantly it dimmed and a few of the surrounding leaves dimmed too.

"Careful", said Iola, "They're sensitive."

"Oh, sorry," Cade replied.

"*Hedera Luuminella Arborea!* It's very rare. I was able to take a cutting of a dried up plant and rescue it. I found it one day, many years ago, deep in these woods. I was able to save it and it grew into what you see now." Informed Iola.

Cade again was amazed. Iola smiled.

"Now Cade, we are here to further your training. You have only tasted ever so briefly the ability you possess. With my help, we will unlock all that is within you. It will take focus and strength of mind. Don't be led by what you see, or by what you think you know, but rather, feel it inside you. It will allow you to see beyond what you can naturally see, enabling you to do what is otherwise impossible." Said Iola. "The practice of alchemy has many dimensions and can lead you down paths that are hard to get back from. Don't let it lead you, master it. Remember, everything has an opposite. Hot/cold, wet/dry, good/bad. The temptation is always there to experiment deeper and darker, but the aftertaste it will leave can be deadly."

Cade nodded.

"So, where do we begin?" Iola said brightly. "Alchemy isn't just about manipulating the elements individually, but also combining them and interchanging them. For example, take this seed. By itself, it's just a seed, but add a little earth and water and..." Iola said, as she put a small seed in the palm of her hand along with a handful of dirt, then sprinkled a little water on it.

The small mound of soil began to move, ever so slightly, as a tiny shoot started to grow. In a moment the shoot split into two small leaves, which unfolded as it continued to grow. Roots started to dangle down from her hand as the shoot grew into a stem and a flower bloomed.

"See, each one needed the other. The seed needs earth, and the earth needs water, together they work with each other to produce something greater than themselves." Iola continued.

Cade poked at the flower in her hand, "Imposs...", then he caught himself, "Can you teach me how to do that?"

"Watch and learn, Cade. Watch and learn." She replied. "Of course this is small scale. I'm gifted more with Earth than the other elements. In fact, I helped my father in growing this forest. It took many years, but together we sped up the process. However, there is still more we need to do, as we are not finished yet."

Iola put the flower in a clay pot that was on the table. "All the elements can work together, *do* work together. Being able to combine them takes practice and patience. It can give life, and it can take life away. Always, always give life. Save and preserve for the greater good." She insisted.

Cade suddenly thought of his father and his mother and sighed. The words of his Grandpa swirled around his ears. Something inside him began to boil. All that had happened, all that he had heard, all that was expected of him, it all came to a head.

"For the greater good! FOR THE GREATER GOOD!!" he yelled out. "How many times have I got to hear that? Is this good? Is what I'm doing here GOOD? I'm expected to learn all this stuff in such a small space of time like it's a walk in the park! Then go off and save the day, like I'm some kind of Luke Skywalker!" He continued.

"Cade, it's ok. I know this may seem overwhelming..." Iola said, trying to bring some comfort.

"Huh, Overwhelming! OVERWHELMING! May seem like it's overwhelming?" interrupted Cade.

"I'm not the enemy here Cade, I'm here to help you..." Iola interjected.

"I was living a perfectly good life before...before the White Tree," Cade ranted. He looked down and saw an axe.

"Cade, no!" cautioned Iola.

But Cade had already picked it up.

"It won't do any good." She said grabbing his arm.

But Cade pulled his arm free. "Leave me alone," he said with tears in his eyes,

Iola stretched out her hand, "I can't let you do this."

Cade reached for the door, but Iola made the wood entwine with itself creating a barrier, preventing him from opening the door.

"Let me out!" he demanded.

"Cade, you're upset. Please put the axe down. Think about what you're doing." Said Iola.

"Sorry," replied Cade as he caused the earth beneath them to shake.

Iola tumbled to the floor as the bottles and pots fell off the shelves. One hit her on the head, knocking her unconscious. Cade then turned and used the axe to burst his way through the door and ran towards the White Tree.

His adrenalin was through the roof. All the emotion that he had kept locked up, was exploding like lava from a volcano.

In anguish, pain, and anger, Cade swung the axe with all his might at the base of the White Tree, yelling as he vented. However, the axe just bounced off the tree without leaving so much as a mark. Again he swung.

"None of this should have happened." He shouted, "None of it! You took my Father; you took my mother. I did not even know her. I did not even get to know her. You took what I loved and took it away!"

With every sentence, Cade swung at the White Tree. Sparks flew each time and the axe just bounced off, causing his hands to sting.

"I want them back, I want them back!" he yelled, as he swung again. This time the axe head shattered like glass. Cade crumbled to his knees in tears. "I just want to go home..."

"Cade." A soft familiar voice came from behind him.

He turned, eyes red and full of tears, and buried himself in the arms of the voice, surrendering himself, "Grandpa," he cried.

"It's alright, Cade, ma boy." the voice said as he caressed the hair on Cade's head. "It'll be alright. I'm here."

Those words to Cade were like hot chocolate on a cold winters day, soothing and warming.

"Cade, I understand how this has been hard for you to digest. So many changes. So much to learn. But there's a strength in you, stronger than you realize. I knew that the moment I saw you. And seeing you here, gives me hope, and that hope gives me joy, and that joy gives me strength." He encouraged.

Cade looked up and wiped his eyes and nose. Though the voice sounded like his grandpa, it sounded stronger, and when Cade saw his face, he saw his grandpa's face, but younger.

"Hey, there." Said Cadarn.

"Grandpa?" questioned Cade.

Cadarn smiled the smile Cade knew and loved, "Not yet. This I believe, belongs to you." as he handed Cade his staff.

"Thanks." Cade said, "Oh no, Iola."

"She's ok, no real harm done. Who'd you think gave me your staff?" reassured Cadarn, "Hey, she has brothers. It's not the first time she got in a tumble with one of us."

"Still, I should never have…" Cade said

"Now, now." Interrupted Cadarn, "None of that. Don't go beatin' yerself up. Sure, you should never, but it 'appened, and she's ok, and holds no grudge. Not like you meant it to 'appen anyways. She forgives you. Oh, she wanted you to 'ave this." Cadarn handed him a seed, which made Cade smile.

"Well, just one more lesson." Cadarn said, "Just don't go off and start yelling eh," he teased, "'Ere, put your hand 'ere on the Tree."

Cade did as he was instructed.

"Now say this." Said Cadarn, "Agor."

Cade gave Cadarn a, 'are you serious?' look and said, "Agor...that's it, just say the word 'Open'!?", as the portal opened for him.

Cadarn and Cade embraced each other, "Thank you" said Cade,

"You are the greater good," whispered Cadarn into Cade's ear, "You are the greater good."

Cade turned and stepped into the White Tree and the portal closed behind him. He was alone. Slowly he walked to the center of the room and looked up. He could almost see the very top of the Tree. At that moment, he knew what he had to do. He raised his staff with both hands, then plunged it down into the floor of the White Tree, piercing tree and stone. Suddenly the whole tree shook as lightning flashed from all sides. Cade kept hold of his staff. Then seven bolts of lightning focused themselves onto Cade's staff. Cade let out a cry but could not let go. Then everything went dark and Cade slumped to the floor.

THE WOODEN HUT

Chapter 13

❧ DARKNESS ❧

It was dark. He fumbled around on the floor, searching with his hands, trying to find something, anything that could help him, but he found nothing. He called out, but his voice just echoed and bounced off the walls, only to return empty, for no other ears could hear him. Picking himself up he groaned, as every muscle in his body ached and cried out in pain. "Keep it together," he said to himself as he sat back down. "This is not a time to fall into despair," he said to encourage himself. He thought of a line from the old black and white Laurel and Hardy shorts he used to watch as a kid, 'This is another fine mess you've gotten me into', except he had done this himself. The thought made him chuckle though.

It was scary not being able to see when your eyes were wide open,. It played tricks with your mind a lot, but he was grateful for a learned and studied mind, for it helped him stay focused. Time seemed to move slowly in the darkness, as there was no way to gauge it. The last memory he had before he was knocked unconscious could not help him either, for he had no idea really when that was, or how long he was out for. Time jumping threw off his internal clock and since he did not have a watch, there was no way to tell.

He stood up and groaned again, holding on to his chest. He was sore. He started coughing, which did not make him feel any better. Each cough sent a painful stab through his chest and lungs. He felt up and down, checking his chest; it felt tender and bruised. "Hmmph, nothing serious", he said to himself. He stretched out and heard the cracking of his bones pop a little, "Ooo", he said, turning head side to side, "that felt good…"

Then he heard a sound.

Suddenly a light broke through the darkness from above. He shielded his eyes for only a moment till his eyes got used to the abrupt bright, but welcom, light invasion. Slowly he lifted his head to see what it was, then something unexpectedly dropped down from above, missing him by inches. He backed up until he felt a wall behind him. He tried to call out but words escaped his mouth. No sooner had the light shone down, it was extinguished as the sound of a heavy wooden lid closed the opening above him. The light was gone. Darkness consumed him once again.

Bryce at least was grateful, even if it was for a moment. That little dose of light breathed hope into his heart. Immediately he started feeling around the walls where he was being imprisoned. His mind started to fire up as he began to realize where he might be. Byne Keep! Bryce knew the place well, he had studied and done a lot of research on the place. He had kept journals of his findings and sketches of what he found there. Along the ramparts of the Southside of the Keep were rows of units about eight-foot deep that were used to store grain and other dry goods. The only real access was from the top, however there were small openings high up on the sides, used for ventilation and at the bottom, one to let the dry goods out, which was closed off by a small sliding door panel, all of which were operated by a pulley system.

Bryce then searched with his hands along the floor in the darkness to find whatever had been dropped from above. His hand bumped into a small cloth bag which was tied at the top. Feeling with his hands he took the bag and opened it. The contents inside felt firm. Bryce put his hand into the bag and brought out one of the items and held it to his nose; it was bread. "Thank you," he said, and took a bite. He checked the bag again, each time bringing out something different - dried meat, apples, a type of cheese, more bread. Bryce ate his fill, grateful to whoever gave him this banquet.

Hours later the door above opened again, and Bryce went to shield his eyes. However, this time the light outside did not flood the place like before, was not so bright. 'It must be nearly night', Bryce said to himself. Suddenly hay and straw rained down from above, a lot of it, then the hole closed up again. He heard the door panels open above him then the one at ground level was unlocked and opened. A small pouch dropped through the opening, and then the door panel quickly closed and was secured again.

Bryce got up and went over to where the pouch was dropped; it was water! He opened it and drank it. He had not realized just how thirsty he was. It was cold and refreshing, yet he could not help being a little puzzled but he was grateful for these 'gifts'. He quickly made use of the hay and straw by making a bed pile for himself to sleep in and to sit on. As he was doing so, his thoughts turned to his wife, Maelona.

When they were young they would go on long walks in the hills of the Welsh countryside, when one day, they came upon a haystack, where they took a rest. The days were long and lazy. Love and laughter filled the air. Bryce had been working with her Father for a short while, back in the days when he had hair on his head. In fact, it was Kai that introduced Bryce to his daughter, and the two were like peas in a pod. Kai used to tease Bryce back in the day, that he was supposed to be working for him, not his daughter. But Kai knew what was happening and Bryce had his blessing.

Bryce shifted himself on the straw. "I'll find you still", he whispered as he looked up into the darkness.

DARKNESS

Chapter 14

❧ THE MAN IN BLACK ❧

Cade opened his eyes and stood up. Something was different. The White Tree seemed brighter. Now, in the quiet, he could hear the faint humming sound coming from the veins of lightning that pulsed up and down within the walls of the Tree. Everything around him seemed more alive. He could see it, he could hear it and he could sense it, there was resolve in his eyes, he was ready.

"Show me my father", he said.

Then, like an old television screen warming up, a scene of his father came into view before him. He saw his father in a dark room with little to no light and he was pacing around inside. Cade's eyes started to moisten, "Dad!" he called out. Then Cade noticed something. His father stopped dead in his tracks and looked around for a moment as if he heard something.

"Dad!" Cade called out again.

Again, his father looked around, as if his eyes were searching for something.

"Cade?" his father said softly, "is that you?"

"Dad! Dad! Can you hear me? Yes, it's me! It's Cade dad!" Cade shouted excitedly.

"But how? Where are you? How'd you get here? Is it safe…" Bryce asked, a little bewildered.

"I'm here in the Tree, the White Tree, dad. I'm coming, I'm going to rescue you. You and…. you and mother." Replied Cade.

Then the scene faded.

"NO!" shouted Cade, "NO! Bring him back, bring it back…" as he thumped on the inside wall of the Tree, with tears in his eyes, but it was gone. Cade hung his head and exhaled. "Take me to him", he whispered. Then Cade heard the portal open, he turned his head, grabbed his staff and stepped through into the portal.

Cade found himself surrounded by trees. The forest was a lot older now and more established. The trees were tall and thick and the forest floor was covered with ferns and other woodland plants. Cade breathed in the forest, as he looked around cautiously. The air was crisp and cool in what seemed like the early morning. Fog was slowly drifting across on top of the trees and an eerie stillness hung in the air. Cade closed the portal door and made his way into the forest.

From what he could tell, no one had been to this part of the forest for a very long time, as there were no trails or any other signs of disturbance in the undergrowth. Cade was rediscovering the forest he once knew, for the first time. A little deeper into the forest, he came across a huge tangled web of bushes and ivy growing over the remnants of an old fallen tree, which was now mostly decayed. He stopped for a moment, surveying the area. 'Could this be...' he thought to himself. He waved his hand and the tangled mess of bush and ivy weaved itself apart and formed a tunnel. Cade smiled. 'Iola's wooden hut', he said to himself, 'it's still here'. With excitement in his eyes, he ducked down and made his way into the tunnel. It went a lot further back than he remembered, but then it had not been accessed for many years. He was amazed to see the door still intact, he gave it a tug and it opened. The room seemed to take a breath, which was something that it had not done in many, many years. Inside it was dark and smelled of old dry wood. As he lifted his hand above him, he touched something that brushed against him. Suddenly, like clouds clearing in the night sky, a green/yellow light started to illuminate the whole place. The luminescent ivy covered the entire area, as it had completely taken over the hut, with vines hanging from the ceiling and running across the floor and walls. The sight was quite breathtaking.

Cade made his way inside, moving the ivy out of his way like bead curtains, and searched the table and shelves, though he did not really know what he was looking for. Everything was covered in wood dust, the bottles and clay jars on the shelves were cracked and empty. It did look like something had happened here. In fact, it looked like the place had been ransacked, because on closer inspection, things were broken, torn down and littered across the floor. Cade also noticed that this was not the work of some small rodent or animal, it had the hallmarks of human intervention. Whoever did this was looking for something, but what? Did they find what they were looking for? Who else would have known about this place?

These were the questions bubbling up in Cade's mind when another thought struck him, Iola had given him a seed. He cleared a space on the table and grabbed a handful of soil, then opened the pouch tied to his belt and retrieved the seed he was given and planted it in the soil. All he needed now was some water. He looked around and noticed some moss growing from one of the walls that had water droplets slowly dripping down from it. Cade collected some of it, sprinkled it over the seed and sat back. The soil started to move, as a small shoot appeared, which grew into a mushroom. As the mushroom opened up, it released a cloud of spores into the air, like smoke from a chimney, which started filling the place. The spores danced and swirled about in the air around him, forming shapes and shadows. Soon a whole scene appeared and played before him, like an echo, except this was visual. Cade stood there as the spores captured the moment.

A tall man dressed in black burst through the door. He had short black hair, a thin drawn face and wore a goatee that ended in a point. His features were not sharp enough for Cade to make out clearly who it was. In his hand, he had what looked like a ball of light that seemed to swirl around. With his free hand, he knocked over the bottles and jars on the shelves, picked them up, looked at them, then threw them down again. He was looking for something and the longer it took the more agitated he became.

The man in black turned and looked right into Cade's

face, as if he could really see him, then walked right through him and searched the table. Cade let out a gasp and turned to see what the man in black was going to do next. Under the table was a small chest, no bigger than a shoebox, which was locked. This only irritated him more. He threw the chest on the floor in the hope of breaking it open, but it did not work. Drawing his sword, the man in black began to smash the chest open with the hilt of the blade. After a few blows the chest broke open and a small book fell onto the floor. Sheathing his sword, he picked up the book. He opened it, slammed it on the table and leafed through the pages. It seemed as though he had found what he was looking for because he paused on one particular page.

Cade took the opportunity to see if he could read what the intruder was looking at. It was a formula to siphon the energy from certain elements when fused together. There was mention that this was only possible with the help of some rare crystal stone. Unfortunately, Cade was not able to read the entire process, as the man in black suddenly closed the book and turned to leave. However, before he did, the man stopped in his tracks and turned his head slightly. Tucking the book under his arm, he reached into his pocket, pulled out his balled hand and turned towards

Cade. They both stood there as if they were face to face, then the man in black blew whatever contents were in his hand into Cade's face, which made Cade sneeze as he fell back, a little surprised. He landed on the table, breaking it apart as it crumbled into pieces for it had dry rotted out. Cade was not hurt, though for a moment everything seemed a little foggy. He stood up and dusted himself off. The man in black was gone, the shadowy images were gone, everything was back to the way it was, old, dusty and broken.

Just as Cade was going to leave, he noticed his staff was leaning on a cloak, and what looked like a longbow, hanging up in the doorway. He was amazed that the cloak still looked in great shape, he took it off the peg, gave it a shake or two and put it on. The cloak fitted him like a glove, as if it was made for him. Next, he took the longbow and pulled on the bowstring a little, it felt firm and stable enough to use. He looked around for some arrows but did not find any. Cade went to put the bow down, but something inside his mind told him to shoot the bow. He lifted the bow up and pulled the string back then let go. As he did, a shadowy arrow appeared as it flew through the air hitting the side of the hut. Cade jumped and looked unbelievingly at the arrow and walked up to it. As he went to touch the arrow it turned into a puff of smoke and disappeared, leaving just the hole that it had made in the wall. Cade stood there and marveled. He put it over his head and rested it on his shoulder. Cade grabbed his staff and left the hut.

Once outside, the temperature had dropped. A cold chill blew through the trees. Cade knew that he had quite a journey ahead of him, he pulled the hood of the cloak over his head and started his way towards Byne Keep.

Chapter 15

❧ THE WALLED VILLAGE ❧

The winds had picked up by the time Cade approached the edge of the forest. It was wintery cold making his breath vapor in the air. He was grateful for the extra layer, as the cloak shielded him from the blowing wind. Cade looked up into the sky, the clouds were grey and heavy, ready to give up their load. He pulled the hood of the cloak over his head and trudged on. Byne Keep stood in the distance, partially hidden by the rising freezing mist, overlooking its territory. Cade noticed something that was new to him, Byne Keep was surrounded by what looked like a tall wooden wall that descended down and around it. He could also see small rooftops and some other tall structures poking out of the mist.

About an hour later, the winds died down, but it was still cold. Cade was getting tired. Trekking through the forest, rolling grasslands and hills was beginning to wear him down, and now he was hungry. Remembering his camping days with his dad, he began to forage the land in search of something to eat. In a short time, he found some edible berries and tree nuts to eat, which gave him the burst of energy he needed. After he had eaten enough he stored some away in his pouch pocket for later and carried on his way.

Shortly afterward, Cade came across a dirt road, which led upwards, so he decided to follow it. Soon he encountered people on donkeys carrying empty sacks, which were rolled up and tied together. Some of the donkeys were pulling carts behind them, some of which were empty, while others coming from the opposite direction were carrying various materials. Most did not pay him any attention, though a few just looked at him as they rode past. The closer he got, the more traffic there was travelling back and forth. Then there it was. Standing about fifteen feet high, stood a grand and heavy wooden gated entrance with large iron clasped gates. The towering walls, large and thick, separated the worlds of those who lived outside and those who lived inside.

As Cade approached the gated entrance, he tried not to look nervous. They were checking everyone who left and entered the walled village. Cade stood in line behind one of the carts while the guard searched it. They cleared it to go inside. Next it was Cade's turn. He stood there a little unnerved, but stepped forward.

The guard was about six-foot tall, strong and intimidating with a square shaped head with thick dark eyebrows and eyes that seemed to look right through you.

"What's your business here?" the guard asked in a deep rough voice.

Cade hesitated.

"Come on, state your fare," the guard was getting impatient.

"I'm…. I'm…errr," Cade began to say

The guard shoved him, "What's the matter with you, hiding something?" he insinuated, about to arrest him right there on the spot, then he noticed the staff in Cade's hand.

"What you got there?" The guard said taking it from Cade.

"No… no… please, that's mine," Cade spoke up

"So you do have a tongue!" The guard teased, "What you do? Steal it?" as he went to motion with his hand to call another guard.

"No. No, good sire. I. I made it." Cade blurted out.

"Made it, you say." the guard replied, "You a carpenter?"

"Yes, sire. I am, good sire. Please, I'm just..." Cade said

"Just a little timid" the guard interrupted him, "Hmm, you carpenters are all the same." He said with a smirk, "here you go." returning the staff back to Cade. "Get yerself, in 'ere. By the looks of it, you a fine craftsman. We could do with some of that. Meet me back 'ere at sundown. I got a job for you."

"Thank you, good sire. I'll be here." Cade replied and walked through the gates and into the walled village.

People were everywhere, buying and selling, making and mending, running this way and that. To the left near the gates was the stall for the donkeys, which were being tended by the keepers, next there were small livestock pens and paddocks, holding chickens, pigs and goats.

There were buildings of every trade from blacksmiths to stonemasons, butchers, bakers and chandlers, all nestled around the main central area. The buildings themselves were all made of wood, with the beams exposed on the outsides, there was a pasty material between them, that looked like it was made from a mixture of mud, clay and straw.

Cade was amazed by what he saw. It all seemed like he was in some kind of medieval town at a fairground, or walking through a movie set, but it was real. He was actually here, living and walking in times past, in the present.

"Git yer 'ed out the clouds, boy!" A voice shouted out, as a small cart full of barrels almost ran him over.

Cade tumbled back and bumped into a man carrying a basket of loaves above his head, knocking the man and the bread onto the dirt ground. This then set off a donkey that jumped up and kicked a cart full of apples, toppling them all over the place. The apples then rolled over to where the goats were being guided into their pens, but they rushed out towards the bounty of apples that had spilled on the ground, sending the apple owner and the goat herders into a frenzy. The lull of the day was now full swing chaos. Goats were running everywhere which caused even more problems. People started yelling and screaming while chasing the goats this way and that, while others were trying to gather the apples back before they were eaten, stolen or crushed. One of the goats then chased the donkey, so it ran off towards the chicken coop, causing the poor chickens to run for their lives with feathers flying everywhere, adding to the fiasco.

Cade could not believe this all happened so fast. He ducked down out of the way, watching it all unfold and trying not to laugh, when all of a sudden, a big hand grabbed him from behind.

"We all help each other here, boy!" A voice boomed, "Get to helping." It was the guard he had met earlier and he was not happy.

The townspeople ran about chasing the goats and chickens as they ran wild, in and around the buildings and alleyways, grateful for their new found freedom, while others grabbed the apples and bread that had fallen onto the ground. Cade went after one of the goats, in the process he took a mental note of the entire place. There was the outer area where all the townspeople worked and lived, then there was the inner area, where Byne Keep stood, towering over everything. The Keep entrance had two thick, heavy iron clasped doors with a portcullis above it. Two guards were outside guarding the entrance, one on the right and one on the left, with two more on the inside. The Keep itself was surrounded by its own fortified wall, which was made of large round timbers with pointed tops. A wooden bridge about ten feet long, sloped downward from the Keep entrance, which led to two mini towers on each side of the bridge and the fortified wooden wall. A guard stood on each of the mini towers, which were about ten feet high, they were armed with a bow and a spear. It was well guarded and getting in was going to be difficult, though Cade did notice that people were being allowed though, if they had business inside Byne Keep. Somehow, he had to come up with a plan to get himself inside, so he could then rescue his parents, without being caught in the process.

It took about half an hour to restore the peace again. Cade caught the goat he had been chasing and walked back to the village area holding onto the goat's horn. The rest of the goats were finally rounded up, the chickens were ushered back in their coop, the apples, what was left of them, were gathered up and put in a barrel, while the broken and half eaten ones were separated. The bread suffered the most loss, as they had been trampled upon both by man and animal in the fray.

The sun was setting and it was getting dark. The bustle of the day was coming to a close, Cade returned the goat and made his way back towards the town gates to meet up with the guard who had told him to meet him there.

"Been quite a day for you eh?" A voice said behind him.

It was the guard he had met twice already that day. "Always something going on 'ere, though today was a little outta the ordinary." He said looking down at Cade as he bent down and whispered in his ear, "these folk sees a lot. Speaks of it too. Best not to get yerself noticed, if you can 'elp it. What's done is done." He lowered his voice even more, "I been waiting for you."

"Well now", he said speaking up, "come along with me. Like I said, I's got a job for you, we be needing a good craftsman. Come now, ain't got all day!"

Chapter 16

❧ SIR ELIDYR ❧

The fire crackled and popped, warming the air around them. The flickering light of the flames caused shadows to dance around the room. The guard took off his gloves and laid them on a table. Cade sat there in a high-backed wooden chair in front of the fire, amazed that he was actually inside of Byne Keep. The guard that brought him in seemed to hold authority, as they just passed by the guarded wooden bridge and into the Great Square of the Keep with just a nod of his head. No one questioned him. They walked straight in. While they were inside, a guard walked over to him and handed him some papers, while taking a quick look over at Cade. They exchanged some words, which Cade could not hear, then the other guard looked over again at Cade, they parted ways and the guard that brought him there led him to his own quarters.

"Ain't too comfortable here. But the fire helps. The name's Sir Elidyr, one of the last Knights of this 'ere place. I'm getting old and I'm tired, I've seen too many things. Many things I now regret. Was about to give up hope, then you came along, just like she said." He continued.

Cade looked up at Sir Elidyr surprised.

Elidyr continued. "I served the then Baron, Baron Arthus of Smythe, he was a smart man, shrewd yes, but a leader of the people. I had served him many years up North before we came here to Wales, returning to the Baron's ancestral roots. He had two children, his daughter, Seren, and his son, Maxen. Sadly, Baron Arthus had lost his daughter due to a barn fire, many years ago. His son, born three years after her death, grew and became strong and learned, just like his father. It was his idea to come here and he had pleaded with his father to return to these parts. Well, as young men do, he fell in love and married a young girl. Sadly, months later, Baron Arthus got sick and died suddenly. Now a new Baron was in power, the only heir of Arthus, -Maxen. That's when everything changed. Everyone thought he was in mourning, but that was not so.

A darkness had awakened in him, revealing who he really was. He was not just the son of a Baron, he was a sorcerer, a dark sorcerer, with many hidden years of teaching. The true reason Maxen had urged his father to come here was to find the Stone of Power, called the Rock of the Celt. However, he found out that a Tree had grown over and around where this rock once sat. Not only that, but this place was being solely used by an Alchemist, who seemed to have claimed it for himself. I don't know how, but Maxen learned that the only way he could link himself to the Rock of the Celts now, was by gaining the Alchemist's trust and marrying into the family. We were all disillusioned, like we were under a spell or something.

"Upon hearing the terrible news that her father and brother fell by the hand of her husband Maxen, she confided in me and told me to wait for the young man with the staff, and described it to me in detail. She said he will be our hope." Sir Elidyr looked down sorrowfully. "She died two years ago. Her name was..."

"Iola. It was Iola, wasn't it?" Cade said mournfully

"Yes, yes it was." Replied Sir Elidyr as he placed a log into the fire. "Years past, Maxen became obsessed with finding this object called the Celtic Oval, then, about several years ago, he spotted a woman with a young child deep within the forest, by a white tree, which was known only to the Baron's inner circle. Somehow she had found what he was looking for and he sent us to capture her but before we could, the child disappeared into this tree.

Maxen had put a watchman near this white tree, waiting, watching, then about a week or so ago a man appeared, a short guy with a beard. He had what the Baron was searching for all those years."

"That's my father!" blurted out Cade as he rose to his feet.

"Hey, quiet down, remember, these walls have ears." Sir Elidyr said.

Cade, with tears in his eyes, slowly sat back down.

"He's safe. They *both* are." Sir Elidyr reassured. "What the people here don't know is that the Baron isn't here, he disappeared into the tree a few days ago. I am the only one who knows this. I am here to help you. I gave Iola my word and I will give my life to it. If you are our hope, I am here at your service. His spell over me is broken. His tyranny must come to an end. I have a few loyal followers of my own and, although I am old, I still have life in me yet. If there ever was a time to save the prisoners, now is the time. We must do this tonight!

"However, the night is still young, so we must wait and

in the meanwhile, get some rest. I'll be back in a short while, I have some business to attend to. Stay here till I return, don't you worry, no one will come to this door." With that, Sir Elidyr picked up his gloves and left, locking the door behind him.

Cade was too wired to rest. The thought of rescuing his dad and seeing his mother, who he did not know, was causing his adrenaline to bubble up inside of him, like a shaken soda bottle, building pressure, ready to pop. He paced up and down.

Sir Elidyr's room was a fair size, with banners and tapestries that hung on the walls. There was a bed off to the side, near the fireplace, and a table in the middle of the room with a few ornate chairs around it. It looked every part a medieval room, as portrayed in history books. Then Cade noticed a collection of swords. Intrigued, he picked one up. It was heavy. Cade held it up as he watched the light of the fire reflecting off the blade. 'Nice', Cade softly whispered to himself. It was a two-handed sword with the hilt wrapped in leather with a round ball on the end; it had some weight to it too.

The blade was about three inches wide at the base, which tapered off to a point. It was about three and a half feet long and was double-edged. Cade swung it in the air and it made a swooshing sound, which made Cade smile and only encouraged him more as he swung again and again into the air. He allowed the weight of the blade to swing him around as he fought imaginary foes until his last swing hit the table and got stuck in it. Cade yanked at the sword to release it. when suddenly, he heard the lock of the door turn and open. He looked over towards the door whilst still trying to get the sword out from being wedged in the table. Sir Elidyr entered and closed the door, "We have to move...now" he said as he saw Cade holding on to the sword which was stuck in the table.

Cade stood there, like a deer in headlights, embarrassed and a little ashamed. "I...I...er" Cade stuttered.

Sir Elidyr walked over to Cade and took hold of his sword, gave it a good tug, and released it from its hold. "A great sword this," he said, with a grin. "seen many a day, it has and can tell many a story, but you're not its storyteller. Come now, the time is upon us." As he sheathed the sword to his side.

It was pitch black outside and the only light was from the cloud covered moon and a few torches that were lit on some of the walls below. It took a while for Cade's eyes to adjust to the low light but he could see enough to follow Sir Elidyr who was in front of him. He led Cade to the south side of the Keep where Cade's Father was being imprisoned.

"I have to lower you down." Whispered Sir Elidyr, "It's not going to be easy to bring you both up, as I'm only one man. We got to do this quickly and quietly, if anything happens you're both going to be stuck down there."

"It's alright," Cade replied, "Let's go."

Sir Elidyr opened up the door on top of the storage pit while Cade wrapped a rope around himself. Cade dangled his legs down into the pit as Sir Elidyr held on to the rope. Cade shoved himself off the edge as Sir Elidyr took the weight and then slowly lowered him down into the darkness. As Cade descended slowly, his staff started to emit a low glow, like those glow sticks you get at fairgrounds, the light ate away at the darkness. When Cade was nearing the ground he dropped his staff and it dug into the ground, "Dad, Dad, it's me, Cade, I'm here." Cade whispered, but there was no answer. Cade reached the bottom and untied himself from the rope. He could see the body of his father on the ground in the hay. Cade ran over to him. "Hey dad, it's me." He whispered again, a little louder this time as he shook him.

Cade's eyes began to fill with tears, "Dad, Dad, wake up!"

"Hey, come on, we don't have much time." Sir Elidyr

quietly called from above.

"Huh!" came a grunt, "Wha...who.... CADE!"

"Shhh!" said Cade. As they embraced, their eyes were wet with tears.

"My son, my son, but how..." Bryce said over and over.

"We don't have much time; we have to get you out of here. Can you stand?" Asked Cade.

"Yes, yes, sure. I can. I've been well taken care of these past few days." Replied his father.

Cade tied the rope around his dad and tugged on the rope. Sir Elidyr slowly pulled him up. When Bryce reached the top, Sir Elidyr helped him out and untied the rope then dropped it down for Cade. As Cade was tying the rope around himself, he heard a scuffle up above. Muffled words were exchanged followed by more scuffling then a body fell down into the pit.

Cade saw the lifeless body in the faint glow as his father called softly from above, "Come, come, you ready? Let's go". Cade grabbed his staff and as he was lifted up out of the pit, the light from his staff faded and returned to normal.

When he reached the top, Cade once again hugged his father.

"Save that for later, we have one more stop. Someone

will be looking for this guard in a short while and we don't want to set off any alarms just yet." Said Sir Elidyr. "Getting to the Baron's Hold will be more difficult, there are three of us now and we'll be more noticeable. Keep your heads low and your wits about you."

The three of them walked in the shadows of the Keep with Sir Elidyr leading the way. The halls were empty and dark until they came near the entrance to the Barons Hold. It was guarded by two guards and lit.

"How are we going to get through them?" questioned Cade.

Sir Elidyr thought for a moment, "Stay here," he said as he walked on over. "Sleeping on the job eh! The Baron won't like that, he'll 'ave you 'ung drawn 'an quartered."

The guardsmen stood to attention a little unnerved. "Sir Elidyr." One of them spoke up. "Our apologies, Sire."

"Keep it to yerselves" he replied, "I got business with the Baron, let me in."

"But..." the guard began to say.

"But....But what? Hold your tongue, and speak not back to me. Open this door or I'll use your 'ed as a battering ram." Demanded Sir Elidyr.

"A battering ram! Is that the best you can come up with?" laughed the guard.

"Well I thought it was a good line, was that not a good line, Arwel?" reasoned Sir Elidyr. And they all laughed.

Bryce and Cade looked puzzled at each other then looked towards Sir Elidyr and the guardsmen.

"Come," Sir Elidyr said, beckoning Cade and his father to join them. "These are my sons, Arwel and Cynfor." They all greeted one another.

"On a serious note," Sir Elidyr continued, "the grains of sand are against us. Let us in and lock the doors, rally the other men together, blood may be shed tonight."

Arwel took the keys and opened the door to the Barons Hold. Cade, Bryce and Sir Elidyr walked inside. Sir Elidyr put his hand on Arwel's' shoulder and looked intensely into his eyes, "Take care of your younger brother," he said softly. Arwel nodded and closed the door behind them.

Chapter 17

✥ THE DRAGON ✥

Darkness engulfed them. The echo of the door being locked bounced all around. The atmosphere was heavy and cold. The three stood there together but alone. Moving, even turning your head seemed difficult, like some invisible force had frozen them in place. Bryce opened his mouth to speak but his words went unheard, even to himself. Sir Elidyr reached for his sword but his hand went right through the hilt and could not get a grip on it. Cade removed his hood and peered into the darkness as if he could see something.

Suddenly there was the sound of a creature snorting through its nose, as a large form loomed up in front of them, revealing the smoky fiery outline of its beastly form.

It towered above them as a molten metallic odor began filling the air. The dark creature raised its huge clawed hand ready to smite them right where they stood, but as it did so Cade held out his staff, releasing a flash of light. The creature turned its head as he swung his hand towards Cade, sending him and his staff flying in opposite directions across the floor.

The creature rolled its head and stomped on the ground sending forth a shock wave, which knocked Sir Elidyr and Bryce off their feet. It snorted again releasing another blast of molten metallic odor into the air. Cade felt along the floor in search of his staff but could not find it. Sir Elidyr reached for his sword again, but as before, his hand passed through the hilt like it was made of water. Cade picked himself up, it was so dark he could not see his dad or Sir Elidyr; he called out, but his words were unheard.

The beast turned in Cade's direction and let out a roar sending a spew of toxic gases and fire in his direction. Cade turned covering his head with his cloak. He could feel the force of it, but it did not harm him, the cloak seemed to absorb it all. Then the beast stopped as if to take a breath and Cade remembered the bow he was carrying. He took it from around his shoulder, pulled the string back and let go. A fiery arrow appeared as it flew through the air towards the body of the shadowy creature. The arrow struck the arm of the beast causing it to flinch in pain. Cade looked at the bow, surprised, then looked again at the creature, as he pulled the string back again, releasing another fiery arrow, hitting the beast in its side. Once again, the beast flinched in pain. Sir Elidyr could see the outline of the creature recoil in pain but did not know why.

Getting to his feet, he felt the weight of his sword by his side, so he reached for it again. This time he could grasp a hold of it. He unsheathed his sword and ran towards the darkness of the beast swinging it as he went. His sword sank into the side of the creature and got lodged there. The beast turned its head towards Sir Elidyr and picked him up with its huge clawed hand, by the scruff of his neck. Cade shot another two arrows at the beast in succession, causing the beast to let go of Sir Elidyr. The beast became angry and turned his full attention towards Cade. As Cade went to release another arrow, the beast swung its tail like a whip, hitting Cade's hand causing him to let go of the bow. Cade's hand was stinging like he had just been stung by a giant bee, only worse.

The creature then stood over Cade and looked down towards him. They were almost face to face when all of a sudden, a bright light burst forth, like the striking of a match on a matchbox. Lightning flashed all around the body of the beast as it recoiled, flailing left and right, letting out the most awful screams. It could not release itself from the tip of the staff, no matter how it tried. Bryce had found where Cade's staff had fallen and had thrust it into the beast. "Leave my son alone!" Bryce shouted, as he pushed the staff deeper into the beast. Then with one final pulse of light, the darkness of the beast dispersed into a million pieces as it let out one last cry and was gone.

Sir Elidyr's sword clanged on the floor as it fell, the heaviness and the darkness in the room was gone and a dim light shone around the room. Bryce was standing up on his knees with Cade's staff in both hands still raised in the air. On the other side of the room, Cade sat, in pain, clutching his hand to his chest. Bryce got up and ran over to his son.

"Are you ok? Let me see," Bryce said to Cade.

"Yeah, I think so," he replied, "it just stings a lot."

Cade showed his dad his arm. There was a three to four-inch welt across his wrist. The skin was not broken, but it was red raw. Bryce tore a bit of cloth from his shirt and wrapped it around the wound and tied it off.

"This should help for now." Bryce said, "But we will need to clean it"

"It's ok dad, really, it's not that bad." Said Cade.

"Ok, son, ok," replied Bryce smiling and patting Cade on the shoulder. "Come, we have to find your mother."

Cade looked into his Father's eyes and nodded slightly.

"Don't want to come across whatever that was again!" Sir Elidyr said as he picked up his sword.

"You got that right." Said Bryce.

"We have to keep moving, the Hold is over here, this is where Baron Maxen had us bring the prisoner." Said Sir Elidyr.

"What!" shouted Bryce, grabbing Sir Elidyr, "You! You took my wife!"

"No! No, I did not. It was the Baron; it was Maxen." Sir Elidyr replied in a whisper, "Keep your voice down, or we won't get to her before we're captured ourselves.

"Listen, I know this is hard for you both, but you got to understand, I did not know then what I know now. I was under the influence of the Baron, I was here to serve him and to do his bidding, but then...then I saw her for myself. It was as if I had seen a ghost. I...I saw the eyes of Iola in this prisoner. It unlocked something in me. A promise I had made, many years ago, resurfaced. I told her I would help her when the time was right and that time has come upon us. This prisoner told me about you, Bryce, that's why I came to your aid when I had the chance. There was little that I could really do, but the little I could, I did."

Bryce loosened his grip from Sir Elidyr, "Forgive me...I"

"No forgiveness is necessary. I am indebted to you... to you all." Interrupted Sir Elidyr.

Suddenly a commotion was heard on the other side of the door.

"Come," said Sir Elidyr, "we must go".

They went over to the Hold but found nothing, no one was there.

"Is there another place the Baron would have taken her?" Asked Cade.

"I don't know, I...," replied Sir Elidyr.

There was banging on the door with loud voices behind it.

"What are we going to do?" Said Cade, "we're trapped!"

"I can take many a man down, but I don't know if I can take them all." Sir Elidyr said.

Bryce looked around, "I don't think that is going to be necessary," he said as he found a particular stone and pushed on it. Immediately the wall moved and revealed a hidden entrance. "Go quickly", he said.

Cade, Sir Elidyr, and Bryce went through the door. Once they were though, Bryce pushed on the other side of the stone and the door closed tight.

"They won't find us here," Bryce said, matter of factly. "This was not discovered until the fall of the Keep. We're quite safe now."

The passageway was small and dark, there was a faint glow coming from the other end. As they made their way, they came to a small winding staircase, which led down to a large well-lit room. What they saw amazed them all.

Riches! Gold and silver piled everywhere. Precious stones and fine cloth lay over the tables and the floor. The walls sparkled and glistened from the light reflecting off the gold and jewels, like a disco ball. It was quite mesmerizing. "Look at all this." Said Sir Elidyr, as he ran his hand through one of the piles of gold coins, then his glove got stuck in the pile. He managed to get his hand out of the glove just in time before the pile of gold coins seemingly consumed it. "What the...?" said Sir Elidyr.

The piles of gold and silver rattled and came together along with the fine clothes and robes that lay all about, taking on a dragon-like form. It stood there, with its head reaching the ceiling, its tail swishing back and forth and had its wings tucked in against its body. But something looked wrong. Something seemed to be in their favor. It had no eyes, it could not see. Cade motioned to his father and Sir

Elidyr to move slowly, somehow they had to get around this dragon-like creature without being sensed and carry on their journey to find and rescue his mother. Sir Elidyr slowly drew his sword and crouched down. He pointed to Bryce and Cade signaling them to carry on while he stayed and faced the dragon. Cade shook his head, but Sir Elidyr insisted as he suddenly yelled out and swung his sword cutting into the neck of the dragon. "Go!" he shouted, "Go now!" Gold and silver coins scattered everywhere as he struck it, only then to regroup themselves back in place. The dragon let out a roar.

Cade and Bryce ran behind the dragon into a hallway and turned the corner. They could hear the sounds of the coins falling to the ground, as Sir Elidyr swung again at the dragon. "We can't just leave him by himself," Cade said to his dad.

"Son, listen to me. He is staying behind so that we can find my wife.... your mother." Bryce said reassuringly, "Come, he is buying us time." They ran along the narrow hallway only to come to a dead end.

"No, this can't be right," said Bryce as he felt all along the walls, searching.

He found nothing.

He sat with his back against the wall, discouraged. "I

just don't understand, Cade. I...I guess she's not here." Bryce said sorrowfully with tears welling in his eyes.

"It can't be. She must be." Said Cade, as he knocked on the walls with his staff. "There has to be somethin...." Cade's staff penetrated through one of the walls.

"Did you see that, dad? This wall isn't a wall, it's not solid." Cade said enthusiastically, tapping it again. This time the wall rippled like water. He tapped it again, only harder this time, "look, dad, are you seeing this?"

Bryce got to his feet. Cade swung his staff like a baseball bat and as it hit the wall, it shattered like glass, revealing a small room behind it and there sitting on the floor in chains, was his mother.

THE DRAGON

Chapter 18

&. FALLEN .&

Bryce ran over to his wife Maelona, and held her tight in his arms, as Cade stood there in silent wonder, his mind numb. "My love, oh how much I've missed you," Bryce said tearfully, "I'm here now, we're here now. This...this is our son," he continued, pointing over to Cade.

"Mum..." Cade said softly.

His mother looked up, her eyes full of love and happiness, and beckoned him to come over. All three kneeled in a huddle, crying tears of joy.

"Here, let me help you with these chains," Cade said as he took hold of them. The solid iron chains turned to rust in his hands and crumbled into dust.

Bryce whispered, "that's amazing...how...you just..."

"Dad, we have to go", said Cade with a smile, "we have to get out of here."

"Yes, yes of course. Maelona, are you fit enough to walk?" said Bryce.

Maelona replied, "Bryce, seeing you again, and my son, has given me the strength of a thousand horses." she smiled. "I'm ready to return home."

Bryce, Maelona and Cade left the small prison room and entered the hallway. As soon as they did, the walls began to shake violently. The stones in the walls and ceiling started to shake loose and fall, smashing into pieces.

"What's happening?" yelled Bryce.

"We have to get out of here," said Maelona, "Seems like the Baron doesn't want us to leave."

They ran back the way they had come to where Sir Elidyr was fighting the dragon made of gold coins and other precious metals. Large stones continued to fall from above.

"Watch out!" said Bryce.

The dragon turned around towards Bryce as he yelled out. Just as it was about to open its mouth, the ceiling caved in on top of the dragon, sending a spill of coins everywhere.

Sir Elidyr said, a little surprised, "Ah, it put up a good

fight.", then saw the three standing together, "I see you found your treasure! Great to see you again, young maiden." He said with a smile and a bow, "Guessin' we can't go that way, come let's face the fray".

Bryce, Maelona and Cade climbed around the fallen stones and the rubble to make their way back to the stairway. However, just before they could get to it, the stairway collapsed sending a cloud of rock dust over them.

"We're trapped, we're trapped." Said Sir Elidyr, "there's no other way out. Ending my days by a falling rock, where's the honor in that?"

Cade called to his dad, "Is there any other way -you know this place?"

Bryce thought for a moment.

"What's behind this wall?", Cade asked.

"Oh, er...oh the stables! The stables are there." Replied his Father.

Cade stretched out his hand and mentally flipped through the pages of the books he had studied with Mael. The wall began to crumble and turn to dust as a hole appeared large enough for them to escape through.

"Quick, let's go", said Cade.

Bryce, Maelona and Sir Elidyr ran through the hole followed by Cade. No one noticed the rattling of gold coins behind them.

Things were no different here, the horses were startled by all the commotion and were kicking while trying to release themselves from their rope ties. Maelona went up to one of them and stroked its mane and the horse instantly calmed down. She untied it and the horse ran free. There were other horses, some had already bolted, some were scared and standing up on their hind legs. Once again, with one touch, each horse calmed down.

"We cannot stay here, my love." Said Bryce, "We have to keep moving".

Maelona nodded and whistled into the air, the remaining horses in the stalls calmed down, she clapped her hands and the ropes dropped loose allowing the horses to run free.

Then the shaking stopped.

Night was nearly over, the air was cold as snow began to gently drift down. Out in the open, Cade, Maelona, Bryce and Sir Elidyr had to find a way out of the Keep. Then the sound of a horn blew loud and long. A battalion of guardsmen rushed into the court of the Keep from every side, all armed with swords and spears. Sir Elidyr mounted one of the horses and unsheathed his sword, "Stay here, stay safe" he said as he galloped towards the guardsmen.

"Men!" he shouted, "We are under attack. Our enemy stands not on the outside of these here walls, but alas here within. For far too long we have seen the corruption plague our people, our families and our lives. We have fought and stood together as one man against our enemies only to ignore and blind ourselves to the truth. The truth of our own captivity and our own enslavement.

"This day I take it back. This day I take my freedom. Yay, not just for me, but for my sons and my daughters. I take a stand against that which has stood against me. Today I say no more. No more will I allow corruption to corrupt me. No more will I be part of it. I am prepared to shed my blood for this freedom. Choose today who you will fight for, the Baron, or for your freedom. For today, I take my freedom, today I become a free man."

One by one, voices shouted, "I will fight for freedom", as they tore the insignias from their attire. Sir Elidyr raised his sword and shouted, "For Freedom!" and galloped off towards the Keep's gates. A resounding cheer came from around the Keep, followed by the clanging of swords as others fought against the revolt.

Cade and his parents crouched down inside the horse's stall waiting for an opportunity to escape. Suddenly, out from behind the stable wall arose a cloud of stone, dust and smoke, followed by a loud screech, as a large golden dragon flew into the air.

Every man froze for a second and looked up into the sky. The dragon circled above Byne Keep twice and perched itself on the roof.

"Run, run for your lives," A voice cried out, "the beast has been released."

At that sound, the dragon turned its attention towards it, jumped from its station and headed towards the man who spoke. Fear gripped the people. They ran to and fro, screaming as they went. The dragon flew and caught the man who had spoken out in its claws and flew upwards. Up and up it flew, then it released the poor man from its grip. The dragon glided on the air currents and turned towards Byne Keep again. Arrows were shot into the air, but they just bounced off the golden coins and the trinkets that the dragon was made of.

There was all-out war everywhere, it seemed like every man was for himself. Then there were those who fought against the golden dragon, others who fought for their freedom, while others fought for the Baron and then there were those who did not know what to fight for.

The dragon would dive down into the Keep and would pick one of the fighting men and throw him into the air as it flew. Then on one occasion the dragon, being blind, missed its footing and slammed into the west wall of the Keep, sending a spray of coins everywhere. Before the dragon could reform, some of the men were able to throw large ropes and cords around one of its legs and wings and pinned it down. However, this only enraged the golden dragon as it spewed out a molten fiery spray from its mouth. Fire then erupted on everything it touched, as the dragon pulled and freed itself from the ropes.

"We have to get out of here." Cade shouted, "If we hang about here, we're toast."

Just then, Sir Elidyr came over to them on his horse, "The gates are open, take a horse and ride to your freedom." He said. "The townsfolk are leaving, now is your best chance."

Bryce and his wife climbed onto the back of one of the horses while Cade mounted another. "Sure you know how to ride one of these?", Bryce asked Cade. Cade just smiled back. All three of them then trotted over to the Keep Gate. Just then the golden dragon swooped down, frightening Bryce's horse. It jumped up onto its hind legs causing Maelona and Bryce to fall off the horse, landing on the stone floor.

"Dad! Mum!" Cried Cade as he jumped off his horse

and ran over to them.

The dragon raised its head as it let out a cry into the air. It flapped its wings and flew up and away, out of sight.

"Sire" came a voice, "we have the upper hand. The Keep has fallen into our hands. Freedom is within our grasp." It was Arwel, Sir Elidyr's son. A huge cheer rang out from the people.

Bryce picked himself up off the floor, a little dazed and bruised. He turned to his wife, "Are you alright?" he asked, "Oh no! You're bleeding."

Sir Elidyr sent for some water.

"Yes, yes. I think so" she replied holding her head.

Cade knelt beside his mum. Water was brought over.

"I'm ok. I'm ok. Really I am." said Maelona.

"Hmm, always the tough one, let me take a look at it," Bryce replied.

He poured some water on a cloth and patted the wound. She winced. "You have a hard head," he said with a half-smile, "Looks like you just got a nice scratch there. But nothing serious."

Cade helped his mum up, "Are you ok to ride?" He asked, concerned.

Maelona smiled and bushed his hair with her hand. "It'll take more than that to knock this girl out. I'm fine.

Come on, let's go home." She replied.

They mounted their horses again and rode towards the gates again. "Well." Said Sir Elidyr, "I guess this is farewell. Be safe on your journey."

Bryce and Maelona nodded, "Thank you, most kindly", they said.

"Yes," said Cade, "Thank you, for everything."

Sir Elidyr put his arm on Cade's shoulder and looked into his eyes, "No, no. Thank you. Take care of yourselves. It's been my pleasu......" he said, stopping suddenly, as an arrow had struck him through his shoulder. Sir Elidyr slumped forward clutching his left shoulder.

"Sir Elidyr!" Cade shouted.

Just then, the golden dragon re-appeared above them, screeching as it flew. The portcullis fell closed in front of them, digging into the ground with force. Laughter echoed all around as the dragon landed in the middle of the court, which stirred up a dust cloud around it. The people scattered in all directions in fear.

Bryce, Maelona, Cade and Sir Elidyr, who was still clutching his shoulder, turned their heads towards the dragon. A black shadow appeared, walking slowly out from amongst the dust as it settled onto the ground. It was Baron Maxen.

FALLEN

Chapter 19

❧ THE BARON ❧

Ahhh, what a glorious welcome! Full of treason and rebellion", The Baron jeered. "tut, tut, tut", he continued, as he wagged his finger side to side. "Let me see now, we have prisoners escaping, the so-called faithful, betraying. My right-hand confidant leading the revolt, and my home, ...my Keep, destroyed and on fire." He said angrily. "Oh and not to mention, releasing the dragon!"

Everyone froze, unable to move. Fear gripped the hearts of every man, as the Baron spoke. No one dared to speak. Then a lone voice shouted out in the silence, "For freedom!" as an arrow flew into the air and struck the Baron on the back, but it just bounced off him. Gasps were heard from all around.

"He who lives by the sword dies by the sword."   The Baron said stretching out his hand as another arrow was released into the air. Suddenly the man who had shot the last arrow was lifted off his feet and flew through the air, faster than lightning, and into the hand of the Baron. The arrow the man had shot struck his own back and the man went limp, "..or in this case, the arrow." The Baron continued, as he let go of the body.

All around was heard the sound of swords falling onto the ground as the guardsmen surrendered themselves once again to the Baron.

"Hmmm, what to do with the unfaithful?"   Baron Maxen questioned, rubbing his chin. "Sir Elidyr! What do you think I should do?"

Sir Elidyr said nothing as he dismounted from his horse. His shoulder was still in pain.

"What is that I see.... a wound! The great and mighty Sir Elidyr is wounded, how...very...sad."   Baron Maxen taunted. "Come, come, dear brother in arms of mine."

Sir Elidyr tried to resist the pull, but found he was no match for the unseen power that grabbed hold of him and dragged him towards the Baron.

"Now let me see here," as he pushed Sir Elidyr to his

knees, "Let me take care of this for you," and pushed down on the arrow.

Sir Elidyr ground his teeth in pain.

"LEAVE HIM ALONE!" Cade shouted out.

"What! Who dares to…ahhh, yes. The young boy I met before. So sorry your grandfather could not make it, but…" Said the Baron as he was interrupted.

"I swear, if you have harmed him, I'll…" Cade retorted.

"Oh! The boy becomes a man in a matter of days! My, my, such foolishness must run in the family." Toyed the Baron. "Such a shame" as he again pressed on the arrow.

"I said leave him alone!" Cade repeated as he stretched out his hand. A gust of wind suddenly knocked Baron Maxen over. Before Maxen could stand on his feet, Cade raised his hands again as chains slithered like snakes on the ground and wrapped themselves around the Baron's legs, arms and body. More and more chains came until all you could see was the top of Baron Maxen's head.

"Cade, that's enough," Said his father.

"But he…" Cade replied

"We're not like him, son. No matter what, that's not who you are." His father continued.

Cade stopped, "OK Father, you're right!" he said.

Smoke started to rise up from the ball of chains

wrapped around the Baron, as the smell of molten metal filled the air. "You want a fight, boy!" The Baron shouted, "You got one!" As he burst free from the bondage of chains.

"Men, listen to me!" Baron Maxen shouted, "Fight for me and your reward will be great. For with every man you strike down, you'll have the strength of two more. We will be undefeated. We will devour those who have stood against us. We shall rise from these ashes and crush the head of our opposed. Just leave the boy to me!"

A darkness began to brew in the skies above, as the snow fell heavier. Men everywhere picked up their swords, however, they did not fight. There was no sound of sword against sword.

Baron Maxen seemed not to notice for he had his eyes fixed and focused on Cade.

"You small minded fool. You're no match for me. Your weak old grandfather was no match for me either. I guess you all want to have a reunion in the underworld...so be it!" Said the Baron as he clapped his hands.

The walls began to shake and tumble all around. Shrieks were heard as stones fell and came crashing down.

Cade crouched down and touched the floor, flipping through pages of the study books given to him by Mael, in his mind. Amazingly, the stones turned into sand as they fell, so that no one got crushed or hurt. Next, he caused the sands to swirl around Baron Maxen, making it hard for the Baron to see or even breathe.

The Baron covered his eyes and his mouth as he stomped on the ground. Immediately the sands fell at his feet but Cade thought quicker. He turned the sand back into stone, encapsulating the Baron's legs in it. In turn, the Baron raised his arms up and a torrent of arrows flew into the air towards Cade. However, Cade was only to look up as the arrows turned to sawdust one by one, like pencils in a pencil sharpener. The Baron raised his arms again, this time every man's sword pointed up in the air, then when he pointed at Cade, the swords flew, one by one, as the Baron waved his arms left and right.

Cade held out his hands. One by one they turned to rust then dust.

"You're not going to win." Said Cade. "You have met your match in me."

Baron Maxen was tired. "You're right, you are right", he said defeated. "Please, spare me."

Cade waved his hand and the stone that held the Baron turned to sand.

"Now wasn't that kind of you, ...you fool!" said the Baron as he pushed both hands out together which sent

Cade flying back and into the wall, like a rag doll. He did it again and Cade was pulled forward and back again into the wall. Again and again, like a yo-yo on a string, Cade flailed back and forth crashing into the walls of the Keep until he had actually broken through the wall.

"No! Stop this!" Shouted Bryce. "You're going to kill him!" as he charged towards the Baron.

Bryce ran with all his might and dived into the air with his arms out. He caught Baron Maxen by surprise as he rugby tackled him to the ground. Both of them landed with a thud. They wrestled on the floor for a moment then Baron Maxen managed to kick him off.

As they both picked themselves up, Cade called out of the rubble to his dad, "Here, catch this," He said, throwing his staff over to his dad. Bryce caught it and swung around, hitting the Baron right on his head. Baron Maxen fell to the ground. Bryce then threw the staff to the side and knelt down by the Baron.

"You have something of ours," He said, as he took the Celtic Oval from his neck. "Don't you ever mess with my family again." He stood and turned to walk away.

"Dad, watch out!" Called Cade as the Baron stood up.

Bryce ducked down and fell forward as Cade release two arrows from his bow.

"You pathetic little peasant, you. You don't have any arrows there, boy!" mocked the Baron.

"Oh but I did!" smiled Cade.

The arrows hit the Baron's wrists, which knocked one sapphire stone off each wristband onto the floor.

During all this time, Maelona was with the Golden Dragon, her touch had kept the dragon still and calm. She whispered into the dragon's ear, "Those are your eyes". The dragon stood up and shook its head, immediately the two sapphire stones placed themselves in their respected place giving it sight again.

The golden dragon snorted and screeched then flew into the air and landed next to Baron Maxen.

"Now, calm yourself, calm yourself." Said the Baron, afraid.

But the dragon opened its mouth and swallowed him whole. It then flew up into the sky. Higher and higher it flew. It dispersed the darkness that covered the skies. It flew higher into the clouds above, disappearing from sight. A large explosion lit up the sky and then there was silence.

Moments later it began to rain. However, what fell from the sky was not water, it was gold. Gold coins and golden trinkets rained from above as people everywhere ran to collect their bounty.

Cade joined his father and mother. "Dad, I never knew you had it in you." He smiled.

"I could not let you have all the fun, now could I?" replied Bryce, "Wow, there isn't a scratch on you."

"Though I feel the bruises, this cape is pretty amazing, it seems," said Cade.

The three hugged each other as the coins kept falling from above.

"I'm guessing you all be leaving now." Said Sir Elidyr.

"Yes, are you going to be alright?" asked Cade

"What, this? A minor scratch, I've had worse," replied Sir Elidyr.

"What about all these people, where are they going to go?" asked Maelona.

"They will find a new place to live. You, on the other hand, have completed your journey here. It is time for you to return from when you came." Said a woman, walking up behind them, robed in a long heavy cloak.

Cade had a puzzled look on his face, then his eyes opened wide as he recognized that voice. He turned around and said

"Iola!?"

Chapter 20

❧ HOME ❧

I t has been many years. It's good to see you again. You, and your family." Said the mysterious woman, as she removed the hood of her cloak revealing her identity. "Yes Cade, I am Iola."

As soon as Cade saw her face, he smiled and ran over to her with arms open wide.

Sir Elidyr looked shocked, "Why...it *is* you...but I thought you had..."

"Brave Sir Elidyr." Iola interjected, "In one sense I did. Maxen was able to cloak me, and my abilities, by the way of transformation. I became enslaved, unable to see or think for myself. I was lost. While in this new form, I found myself blind. All that I once knew was gone, the truth had vanished. What I became, I thought I always was. But I did not like what I was, so I slept and fell into a deep sleep. My next conscious moment I had was when I was awoken." Iola said somberly. "I had no rational thought until...until you", pointing to Maelona, "touched my side. A calmness came over me, a peacefulness. Then your words rang deep inside me, unlockin the hidden truth of who I really was. When my sight returned, all I saw was a black dark beast in front of me, which I knew I had to destroy, before it destroyed all that is known. So using the form I was in, I vanquished the beast once and for all. I am now free." She smiled.

Iola looked over to Maelona, "I know who you are, ...my brother's daughter. How beautiful you are. I see you bear my Father's name within your own." She smiled. "And you sire," looking at Bryce, "The one who stole her heart and blessed our family with your presence. You have a true, strong and noble heart. You searched and found, and fought for your treasure, I know you will always keep her safe." Iola turned to Cade. "And you, young but wise, strong and persistent, your journey has only but begun. Travel it well."

They all embraced each other with tears of joy, yet with a little sadness too.

Cade looked at Iola. "You already know, Cade," she said softly.

Cade looked down at his feet, "You...you are not coming with us, are you?" He asked with tears in his eyes.

Bryce and Maelona put their arms around Cade's shoulders, "Come on son, it's time to go home." Bryce said.

"At least come with us to the White Tree." Cade insisted.

"Yes", She replied smiling, "Of course I will."

Just then, Sir Elidyr was met by his two sons, "What did we miss?" said Cynfor. Placing his hand on his son's shoulder, he replied "Come, my sons, let me tell you a tale like no other."

"Farewell, my friends, farewell." Sir Elidyr said to Bryce, Maelona and Cade, "Oh, just one more thing before you go." Turning to Bryce, he said "This is yours." Sir Elidyr unsheathed his sword and handed it to him.

"But...thank you," said Bryce. "I am truly honored." And bowed his head.

"The honor is ours," Sir Elidyr replied. With that, he turned to his sons. "This tale I'm about to tell, is true." he said as they walked away.

The four of them mounted horses and went to ride out of the Keep but the portcullis was still down. Cade, with staff in hand, just pointed at it and the whole gate aged before their eyes, turned to rust and disintegrated.

"Let's go home." He said.

The four rode out of the fallen Keep and out of the small town area. They galloped down the road then turned into the forest. Finally, they reached the White Tree and dismounted from their horses.

"I guess this is it," Cade said sadly.

Iola gave Cade one final embrace.

"Can I get in on that?" An old voice called out.

Iola froze. It was like time had suddenly picked her up and placed her into a memory of long ago.

"Cadarn...brother!" She said as she turned her head.

Sure enough, Cadarn stepped out of the White Tree and lifted up his hands, "Come now, an old man like me, cannot be waiting all day." He smiled.

Iola went over and hugged him, ever so dearly. "I thought I'd never see you again." She said with tears in her eyes. "Always full of surprises."

Cadarn looked up and saw his daughter. "Maelona, my dear precious Maelona." Maelona fell into the arms of her Father as tears flowed. "I'm glad I got to see you, this one last time." He said as he coughed and coughed.

"But Father!" Maelona cried, "no..."

"My child, my child." He said, stroking her hair, "I am very, very old and my strength is gone. I was able to send Maxen back to you at great cost. I knew you could do it. I knew you all could defeat him. All these years I have carried a heavy burden. The Celtic Oval, though it brought me the best gifts I could have ever asked for, my wife and my daughter, it also became the center of loss.

"I cried many years over the deaths of my father, my brother and my sister. I was no longer worthy to carry my name, so in honor of them, I changed my name to Kai. Wearing the initials of our names gave me solace, if only in part." He coughed again and again.

"Grandpa!" Cade called out.

"Ah, young Cade." He smiled, "though my journey has come to an end, yours has only just begun." And with that, he closed his eyes and went limp in the arms of his daughter.

Deep sobs followed. Bryce carried the body into the White Tree and laid it respectfully down on the floor. Iola, Maelona, Bryce and Cade stood over the body, with great sadness in their hearts. Suddenly the whole place burst with light from where he lay and echoed up within the Tree. Then the light faded and the body was gone.

"He will always be with us," said Iola with a half-smile.

Each one smiled and nodded in agreement.

"I must bid thee all farewell." Said Iola.

They all embraced each other one last time and Iola stepped out of the White Tree.

"Hey, that bump on your head is completely gone!' said Bryce to his wife, "Come to think of it, all my aches are gone too. Cade show me your wrist." And sure enough, when he removed the cloth tie, the wound was gone.

"Amazing," Marveled Bryce, "Absolutely amazing!"

Cade's grandma was waiting for them by the White Tree when they all appeared. What a reunion that was. Both happy and sad. Laughter and tears filled the atmosphere as they walked home together.

"Oh mum, grandpa gave me this, he said it was yours." Said Cade, as he held up a small blue beaded necklace.

"My goodness! I haven't seen this since you were a baby." She said in awe, and put it around her neck.

In that moment, memories she never had, suddenly filled her mind, like the filling of a watering can. They were memories of when Cade was a baby and how Bryce, along with her mum and dad, had raised him. It took her breath away.

"Mum, are you ok?" Cade asked concerned.

She smiled, wiping tears from her eyes, "Yes, my son. I'm fine. My father just gave me a very precious gift."

The End…

————————————

" I sincerely hope you enjoyed reading this book as much as I enjoyed writing it. If you did, I would greatly appreciate a short review on Lulu.com and/or your favorite book website like Goodreads.com. Reviews are crucial for any author, and even just a line or two can make a huge difference. Thank you! "

~Mark

————————————

PHONETIC GLOSSARY

PLACES

Llandyke *(Shhar-an-dye-k)* Wells
Glynn *(Glin)* Hill
Byne *(Bine (as in nine))* Keep
Aberandoen *(Ab-ber-ran-doe-wen)*
Whelhelm *(Well-hem) House University*

CHARACTER NAMES

Cade *(K-ade)*
Bryce *(Br-ice)*
Maelona *(May-yel-lone-na)*
Carl *(K-arl)*
Kai *(K-eye)*
Mael *(May-yell)*
Iola *(Eye-o-la)*
Ardwyadd *(Ard-d-why- yad)*
Cadarn *(Cad-darn)*
Seren *(Ser-ren)*
Baron Arthus *(Are-thus)* of Smythe *(Sm-eye-th)*
Baron Maxen *(Max-zen)*
Sir Elidyr (El-lid-da)
Arwel *(Are-well)*
Cynfor *(Sin-fore)*

ABOUT THE AUTHOR

Mark Christopher Brown is British and a missionary (also he's a bit of a chocolatier too!). He loves science and fantasy fiction, and even played Dungeons & Dragons when he was a kid. After getting an English School education, Mark began travelling through Europe and Africa before flying to the East Coast of America.

He first began writing short children stories, inspired by his family. He has now illustrated these stories and put into print. But his inspiration didn't stop there. One day while out on a walk, he came across a white barkless tree that stood out from among the rest. He was struck with the thought that 'The White Tree' would be a good title for a book. And boom, the novel was born.

Mark Christopher Brown is a husband, a father of six and a grandfather of two.

OTHER BOOKS BY...

Mark C. Brown has written books for children too, inspired by his own sons and daughters. Find the books below on www.lulu.com/spotlight/booksofbrown

GOODBYE/HELLO SERIES *by Mark C. Brown*

A fun story about a squirrel and his animal friends. Discover the changes that happen in Happy Acres Woods from season to season.

Goodbye Spring, Hello Summer   ISBN: 978-1-312-03609-3

Goodbye Summer, Hello Autumn ISBN: 978-1-312-03346-7

Goodbye Autumn, Hello Winter   ISBN: 978-1-312-03319-1

Goodbye Winter, Hello Spring   ISBN: 978-1-312-03627-7

BALLOON ON THE MOON *by Mark C. Brown*
ISBN: 978-1-312-01233-2

A child's fresh enthusiastic look at the world and space, inspired by the adventures of his/her new balloon interspersed with original poems.

ON A FARM FAR AWAY *by Mark C. Brown*
ISBN: 978-1-387-11548-8

A silly poem where the unusual is the norm. Read about a farmer who raises farm animals and grows fruit and vegetables of a different kind.

AFTER THE CREDITS

THE STORY CONTINUES

...Meanwhile back in Whelhelm House University near Seattle Washington in America, Carl McSmythe returned to his dorm. He opened his closet door and took out an old small wooden chest with a round indentation on the lid. The chest was no bigger than a shoebox.

Sitting on the edge of his bed, he laid the small chest down next to him. He took a small key from the rope chain around his neck, unlocked it and opened up the lid. Carl picked up a small leather bound book and an object that was wrapped in cloth and slowly unfolded it, revealing its contents.

"I did it!" Carl said, as he picked up a small golden medallion with a picture of a dragon engraved into it. "He has the stone."

He placed the medallion in the recess on the lid of the chest and turned it counterclockwise. A secret door opened and a small crystal rolled out onto the bed.

"I know what to do," said Carl, "we will be united soon, my Great grandfather Maxen."...